The Mad Catter

by

Kathi Daley

This book is a work of fiction. Names, characters, places, and incidents either are products of the author's imagination or are used fictitiously. Any resemblance to actual events or locales or persons, living or dead, is entirely coincidental.

Copyright © 2015 by Katherine Daley

Version 1.0

They say it takes a village, and I want to thank my entire village for making Kathi Daley Books a success.

I want to start off by thanking my super-husband Ken for allowing me time to write by taking care of everything else.

I also want to thank the very talented Jessica Fischer for the cover art.

I so appreciate Bruce Curran who is always ready and willing to answer my cyber questions.

Special thanks to Vivian Shane, Melissa Nicholson, Veronique Boudreau, Bobby Toby, Maureen Devlin-Murphy, and Janel Flynn for submitting recipes.

And, of course, thanks to the readers and bloggers in my life who make doing what I do possible, especially everyone who hangs out and likes and share my posts at Kathi Daley Books Group Page.

And, as always, love and thanks to my sister Christy for her time, encouragement, and unwavering support. I also want to thank Carrie, Cristin, Brennen, and Danny for the Facebook shares, and Randy Ladenheim-Gil for the editing.

Books by Kathi Daley

Come for the murder,
stay for the romance.
Buy them on Amazon today.

Zoe Donovan Cozy Mystery:

Halloween Hijinks
The Trouble With Turkeys
Christmas Crazy
Cupid's Curse
Big Bunny Bump-off
Beach Blanket Barbie
Maui Madness
Derby Divas
Haunted Hamlet
Turkeys, Tuxes, and Tabbies
Christmas Cozy
Alaskan Alliance
Matrimony Meltdown – *April 2015*
Soul Surrender – *May 2015*
Heavenly Honeymoon – *June 2015*

Paradise Lake Cozy Mystery:

Pumpkins in Paradise
Snowmen in Paradise
Bikinis in Paradise
Christmas in Paradise
Puppies in Paradise

Whales and Tails Cozy Mystery:

Romeow and Juliet
The Mad Catter
Grimm's Furry Tail – *March 2015*

Road to Christmas Romance:

Road to Christmas Past

Chapter 1

Friday, May 29

"Do you think we should let them know we're here?" I whispered to Cody West, my co-choir director, high school crush, and the source of my greatest pleasure and biggest regret.

"No, let's just get the music and go."

I followed Cody down the hall toward the choir room. The previous Wednesday had been my first as the choir director for the St. Patrick's Catholic Church children's choir. Although I was getting used to the idea, initially I'd been less than thrilled to find that Cody would be helping with the choir while he was visiting Madrona Island for the summer. The man brought up conflicting emotions I really didn't want to have to deal with.

"What do you think they were arguing about?" I asked as we entered the small room and began searching for the sheet music we wanted to review before Sunday's service. When Cody and I had arrived at the church we'd witnessed Father Kilian and Mrs. Trexler arguing. The pair had been behind the wall of glass where the confessionals were housed, so while we saw the flaying of arms and the general gestures associated with conflict, we couldn't hear what was being said.

"I have no idea, but I have to admit that I find the whole incident more than a little disturbing."

I had to agree. Father Kilian had been the spiritual leader of the Catholic residents of the small fishing village where I grew up since before I was born. He was beloved by all and considered by most to be the foundation on which the social structure of Harthaven thrived. In all of my twenty- six years I had never seen him raise his voice to anyone. I couldn't imagine what had caused him to become so angry with Mrs. Trexler, a retired third-grade teacher, who, like Father Kilian, is loved and respected in the community.

"You know, Mrs. Trexler has been acting a little odd the past week or so. I stopped by her house on Tuesday, like I always do, but she wasn't there, so I went back on Wednesday before choir practice and she seemed evasive. She was cordial, but she wouldn't look me in the eye. I asked about her trip the previous day and she said she needed to catch an early ferry. She apologized that she hadn't thought to let me know she'd be away because she knew I usually visit on Tuesdays but didn't offer any sort of explanation as to where she'd gone. I was in a hurry to get to the church so I didn't probe, but now I have to wonder if the argument she's having with Father Kilian has something to do with her unexplained trip."

Cody shrugged as he continued to sort through the stack of music. "I don't suppose it's any of our business. Oh, look, I found a piece of music a young Caitlin Hart vandalized."

I looked at the sheet music he was referring to and cringed when I saw the crude drawing across the front of the cover, along with my signature. "I was six," I defended myself. "Six-year-old kids do stuff like that.

Besides, I seem to remember you defiling your own share of sheet music."

Cody winked. "That I did, although my drawings usually weren't G-rated. I imagine the music covers I vandalized were disposed of." Cody paused. "We had fun, didn't we?"

"We did until you decided you were too cool for church choir and quit."

Cody laughed as he replaced the sheet music and continued his search. "I had a reputation to uphold, but I sure do miss those early days in our relationship, before things got complicated."

I didn't say anything. Really, what was there to say? Cody and I had a history. A long and at times messy history. Cody was my brother Danny's best friend when we were growing up. Like many little sisters, I used to tag along with Danny and his friends, and like many big brothers, Danny complained about it to no end. Cody, however, was always nice to me, which was most likely why I developed a huge crush on him the moment I hit puberty.

Looking back, I can see that our love for each other existed only in my adolescent mind. The fact that our devotion was one-sided didn't keep me from making the biggest mistake of my life. When I was sixteen Danny and Cody graduated high school. While Danny planned to remain on the island, Cody had enlisted in the Navy. In a rash act, which can only be attributed to teenage insanity, I decided to seduce Cody on the evening of his graduation in an effort to convince him to stay.

My grand plan worked surprisingly well and we'd shared a magical night. The problem was that instead of staying, as I'd hoped, Cody left as planned, and I didn't see him again until he returned to the island a few weeks ago. It'd been ten years and a lot had changed; my embarrassment, however, was apparently eternal.

"Do you think we should add an extra song to the end of the set?" Cody asked.

"I guess it couldn't hurt. But be sure to choose one the kids already know."

Cody made a selection, added the sheet music to the pile he had already assembled, then closed the cabinet. "I guess this is all we need. Let's head back to your place and have that dinner date you promised me."

"It's not a date," I clarified. "Danny and Tara are coming as well," I added, referring to Tara O'Brian, my best friend. "And we're just BBQing. Nothing fancy."

"Sounds good to me." Cody turned toward the door.

"I need to stop by Bella and Tansy's on the way home. Bella called earlier; she has some herbs she believes will help Maggie recover more quickly and I told her I'd pick them up."

Maggie Hart is my aunt, a feisty woman in her late sixties who is politically outspoken yet locally beloved. She was the front runner in the hotly contested island council race until she became ill several months ago. After months of not knowing what was making her sick we recently learned that someone had been adding arsenic to her tea. Not enough to kill her, but definitely enough to keep her at home and out of the way.

"Okay. Be sure to lock the door behind you," Cody instructed as I followed him into the hall.

As we passed the main body of the church, I glanced inside. Neither Father Kilian nor Mrs. Trexler could be seen in the confession room, and while the building seemed empty, the lights had been left on.

"Hang on; I'm going to get the lights," I informed Cody. "Father Kilian just did a sermon about waste not, want not. I'm surprised he didn't remember to turn off the lights when he left."

I hurried across the room and was about to flip the switch when I noticed something, or I guess I should say *someone*, lying behind the pulpit. I felt my stomach begin to roll as I inched closer to see that the someone on the floor was Mrs. Trexler.

"Cody, I think you'd better call 911." I bent down to check for a pulse, which I already knew wouldn't be found.

Ryan Finnegan—Finn to his friends—is the deputy assigned to Madrona Island. Like many of the island's residents, Finn was born and raised on the northernmost island in the San Juan chain. Once Finn had been engaged to my older sister Siobhan, who broke his heart when she was offered a job in Seattle and left her home and her fiancé without a second thought.

"I need you to tell me everything that happened from the moment you arrived," Finn instructed Cody and me.

We looked at each other. I was reluctant to mention the argument Father Kilian and Mrs. Trexler had been having just minutes prior to her death and assumed Cody was as well. While I couldn't imagine Father Kilian was responsible for killing her, it did seem as if he was the most likely suspect. I wasn't certain the island could survive the upheaval that would occur if Father Kilian was charged with Mrs. Trexler's murder.

"Cait and I came to the church to pick up some sheet music," Cody began. "We found Mrs. Trexler's body on our way out. We noticed that someone had left the lights on inside the church, so Cait went back to turn them off."

Finn looked at me. "Describe exactly what you saw when you entered the church."

I felt shaky, but I tried to focus on Finn's handsome face. He had been like one of the family for so many years. I knew I was safe with him, so I forced myself to relax and try to remember. "I was focused on the light switch when I first entered the room, but something made me turn and glance toward the front of the building," I stammered. "I could see a pair of feet sticking out from behind the altar. I hurried over to investigate and saw that Mrs. Trexler was lying on the floor. Her head was bleeding and there was a candlestick lying on the floor next to her. I yelled for Cody to call 911 and then bent down to check for a pulse. There wasn't one." I took a deep breath. "To be honest, I really wasn't expecting there to be one once I saw all that blood. There was so much blood."

Finn squeezed my shoulder as I struggled to continue.

"I really thought I was going to pass out, but then Cody came over to where I was crouched down and led me to the pews. We sat down in the front row and waited for you."

"Had you seen anyone else in the building since you'd been here?" Finn asked.

"Father Kilian was here when we arrived," I shared. "He was talking to Mrs. Trexler."

Finn frowned. "He was talking to the victim just prior to her murder?"

"He was," I confirmed.

"Do you know what they were talking about?"

I looked at Cody. He shrugged.

"They were arguing. They were behind the glass of the confessional area, so we couldn't hear what they were saying, but the drapes were open and it looked as if their discussion was pretty heated."

"Do you know when Father Kilian left the building?" Finn asked.

I shook my head. "No. Cody and I saw them arguing, so we continued on into the choir room. I don't think either of them saw us. Does Father Kilian know what happened?"

"Yes, he's been informed. He was instructed to wait in his residence until I had a chance to come by to speak with him."

"You don't think . . . ?"

Finn furrowed his brows. "I don't know. I hope not. Is there anything else you can tell me? Did you hear anything while you were in the choir room? A door slam? Footsteps? Anything at all to indicate that someone else was on the property?"

Cody and I both shook our heads.

"Okay, I guess I'll go have a chat with Father Kilian. It might be best to keep this to ourselves until we know what we're looking at," Finn said.

"If Father Kilian killed Mrs. Trexler it's going to be bad," I pointed out. The church was the cornerstone of the predominantly Catholic village. If

Father Kilian was found guilty of murder it was going to destroy something that was already very fragile.

"Yes," Finn agreed. "It really is. I can't believe Father Kilian would do something like this. We need to remember that so far all we know for certain is that they argued."

"I'm sure there's a logical explanation," I stated, even though deep inside I was afraid that what had happened was exactly what appeared to have happened.

"Why don't the two of you head out and I'll call you or come by after I speak to Father Kilian?" Finn suggested.

"We'll be at the cabin," I said, referring to the summer cabin I lived in on Aunt Maggie's oceanfront property.

We left the church and headed toward Pelican Bay. Madrona Island has two very distinct settlements. The fishing village of Harthaven Bay is a functional community with residential neighborhoods, a school, and practical stores such as a market, a drugstore, and a hardware store. It was founded by my great-great-grandfather and eleven other men four generations ago and still is mainly populated by the descendants of the Irish Catholic families who first settled the island.

The community of Pelican Bay has only recently sprung up as a result of the introduction of regular ferry service connecting Madrona Island to the other islands in the area, as well as the mainland of both Washington State and Canada. It's a touristy type village with art galleries, restaurants, B&Bs, and cute mom-and-pop shops designed to meet the needs of our visitors.

Cody and I were headed toward Pelican Bay to pick up the herbs Bella had for my Aunt Maggie. Bella and Tansy own and operate Herbalities, a specialty shop featuring herbal remedies and fortune-telling. I'm not sure either of them are actual witches, but they do seem to know things that, on the surface, aren't really knowable.

Bella and Tansy live in a cute Cape Cod–style house one street off Main. Cody waited in the car while I ran up to the house to fetch the herbs. Normally I enjoy visiting with the insightful women, but today I was anxious to get home to my dog Max and the sanctuary full of cats that I knew were waiting to be fed and tended to.

"I have your packet right here." Tansy handed it to me. "I'd ask you to come in, but I was certain you'd want to get home to Alice."

"Alice?" I asked.

"She'll be by to help."

I was about to try to get more information about Alice, but Tansy closed the door and I realized the name was all I was going to get out of the mysterious woman. This wasn't the first time she'd helped me solve a problem with her cryptic comments, and I was certain it wouldn't be the last.

"All set?" Cody asked as I slipped into the passenger seat of his truck.

"I got the herbs and apparently I'm about to meet someone named Alice."

"Alice?"

"That's what Tansy said. She said I should hurry to get home to Alice."

When we pulled into the drive in front of my cabin I noticed a beautiful white cat sitting on the swing on my front deck. She appeared to be watching the pair of bald eagles that were eating fish left on the beach by the low tide. The cabin I live in is perched on the sand along Madrona Island's west shore, providing a serene and peaceful atmosphere from which to sit and watch the world go by. The cat had picked a perfect spot in which to await my arrival.

"Alice?" Cody asked.

"That would be my guess." I got out of the truck and approached the cat, who wore a blue collar with a silver name tag that identified her. The cat hopped out of the swing and trotted into the cabin when I opened the door. I'd recently played host to a cat named Romeo, who was now living with my next-door neighbor, Francine Rivers, and her cat, Juliet. I doubted Alice would be with Max and me for the long run, but she was a beautiful cat and I decided to enjoy her company while I had it.

"I left Max with Maggie," I informed Cody. "I noticed Danny's truck in the drive as well. I'll go tell them we're back if you want to get the BBQ started. The charcoal and lighter are in the cabinet on the deck."

I headed toward Maggie's house as soon as Cody agreed to my request. It was a beautiful evening, with warm temperatures and clear skies. It would be nice to eat out on the deck. Danny had built me a fire pit two summers back that would keep us warm once the sun began its descent beyond the horizon. I took an appreciative breath of the clean air as I made my way up the steps to Maggie's back door.

"You're late," Danny greeted me as I walked into the kitchen.

"Yeah, I know. There was a situation at the church."

"A situation?" Danny inquired.

I looked around the otherwise empty room.

"Maggie's upstairs with Marley and Tara, looking at fabric."

"Mrs. Trexler was murdered at the church," I said in a whisper. "We can talk about it when we get back to my place. I don't want to upset Maggie until we have all the facts. Let's just get Tara and head over. And I need to stop off to see to the cats."

"Tara and I took care of the cats," Danny informed me. "Maggie came along to supervise. She seems to be doing better. She wanted to handle the chores herself, but Tara and I insisted that she play with the kittens while we cleaned up and fed everyone. At first she insisted on helping, but then this little gray striped kitten wandered over and charmed his way into her heart. I wouldn't be surprised if Akasha doesn't have a new roommate."

"I'm sure she'll love that," I said sarcastically.

Although my aunt is the founder of the Harthaven Cat Sanctuary and has taken on the guardianship of dozens of cats in the past couple of years, Akasha is the only one who lives in the house with her. She's a petite black beauty who adores Maggie but only tolerates everyone else.

"Maggie brought the kitten home," Danny said. "He's upstairs with Marley and Tara. Max is upstairs as well."

"I'll grab Max and Tara," I told him. "Why don't you head back to help Cody with the steaks? I have corn to throw on the grill and a salad all prepared in the refrigerator. I'll just be a minute."

Max ran to the door to greet me as I approached Maggie's sewing room on the second story of the large house. Maggie is the co-owner and -operator of the Bait and Stitch with her best friend Marley. The Bait and Stitch sells both fishing (Maggie's passion) and quilting supplies (Marley's obsession). Akasha was glaring at the room from atop a supply cabinet while Tara sat on the floor with two kittens, her new pet, Bandit, and the gray one from the sanctuary. He really was adorable.

Maggie and Marley were standing near a table on which several fabrics had been laid.

"Oh, good, we can use another opinion," Maggie said as I walked into the room with Max.

"An opinion?" I asked.

"Marley and I are trying to decide which fabric we should use for the quilted sail for our Founders Day float."

Founders Day on the island is a huge annual event that takes place over a three-day period the first weekend in June. It features, among other things, a parade. Local businesses enter floats that compete for prizes. Every year Maggie and Marley went all out to make sure that the Bait and Stitch would be among the finalists.

"I like the royal blue," I offered. "It looks like the sea. Besides, blue is my favorite color."

"It is a nice color," Maggie agreed. "Maybe combined with the tan to represent the sand."

"Are you going with the fishing scene?" I asked. Maggie and Marley had been kicking around ideas for their float for months.

"We are." Marley beamed. "We plan to have two cats sitting in a small boat with a patchwork sail. One of the cats will be fishing and the other will be sewing."

"It sounds adorable. I can't wait to see it." I looked at Tara, who had picked up Bandit and was standing up. "The guys have the steaks on, so I guess we should head back."

"Good. I'm starving. Let me know if you need any help with the float," Tara said to Maggie and Marley. "The remodel on Coffee Cat Books begins on Monday, but I can help out this weekend if you decide to get started."

"Thank you, dear. Your help will be very much appreciated," Maggie said. "I'm surprised you were able to get such a quick start on the remodel. Didn't the loan just come through a few days ago?"

"Yes, but I checked with the bank and the money is available for use. I've had contractors lined up since we began planning the project, so there shouldn't be anything standing in our way at this point."

Coffee Cat Books is really Tara's brainchild, although I'm going to join her as a full half owner. Our plan is to convert the old cannery, which has stood empty ever since it closed down, into a coffee bar/bookstore/cat lounge. Tara is uberorganized and has been working on the project for months. If I know Tara—and I do—she'll have the place remodeled and open by the end of the summer.

"By the way, Bella sent some herbs for you to try. I left them on the kitchen counter," I informed my aunt.

"Thank you. I'll try them before I head to bed. Bella and Tansy are such nice young women. Always looking to help those they can," Maggie commented.

"Yeah, they're great," I agreed.

Tara and I said our good-byes and headed back to my cabin. I'd planned to wait to fill Tara in until we were all assembled, but I never have been able to master the self-control needed to properly time my verbal outbursts.

"Mrs. Trexler is dead," I said as soon as we were out Maggie's back door.

"Dead? How did she die?" Tara gasped.

"She was murdered, and it looks like Father Kilian may be the one who killed her."

"What?" Tara stopped walking. She grabbed my arm and turned to look at me. "You can't be serious."

"I wish I wasn't."

"Father Kilian would never kill anyone," Tara insisted. "You must be mistaken."

I briefly filled her in on what Cody and I had seen as we continued toward the cabin.

"I agree it's odd that Father Kilian was arguing with Mrs. Trexler. I've never seen him raise his voice to anyone. But just because he argued with her doesn't mean he killed her."

"There was no one else around," I pointed out as we arrived at the cabin. The guys were on the deck, overlooking the sea, where the BBQ was set up.

"There has to have been someone you didn't notice," Tara insisted. "What did Finn say?"

"He said he was going to speak to Father Kilian and then come by to fill us in."

Tara let out a deep breath. "I'm sure Father Kilian will be able to clear everything up once he has a chance to speak with Finn."

"I hope so."

"You can't honestly believe he's guilty."

I wrapped my arms around my body as a chill crawled up my spine. I really hoped Father Kilian was innocent, but in spite of my best effort to do so I couldn't quite convince myself that he was as innocent as I wanted him to be.

Chapter 2

Sunday, May 31

As Cody and I got the children from the choir ready for the first service on Sunday morning, I found I was nervous about what the day would bring. Finn had come by the cabin on Friday evening after he'd finished speaking to Father Kilian and reported that while the priest had insisted Mrs. Trexler was alive and well when he left the church, the priest had refused to share with him exactly what it was they'd been arguing about. Father Kilian had informed Finn that the subject of their conversation had arisen during confession, so he wasn't at liberty to talk about it with Finn or anyone else.

Finn had argued that because Mrs. Trexler was dead, Father Kilian was no longer honor bound to keep Mrs. Trexler's confidence, but the priest insisted that the confidentiality of the confessional was eternal. Finn told us that while he didn't have a reason to arrest Father Kilian, he also didn't have a reason to discount him as a suspect. He'd been arguing with the woman prior to her death, and there were no witnesses to his arrival in his home after he left the church other than his cat, Magdalene. I remembered seeing his housekeeper's car in the drive when Cody and I first arrived at the church, but unfortunately, Ms. Winters had left while he was speaking to Mrs. Trexler and so was unable to provide an alibi. To make matters worse, the only fingerprints on the candlestick, which had been confirmed as the murder weapon, belonged to the man no one wanted to believe was guilty of such a violent act.

Yesterday was Saturday, so I'd taken the ferry to Seattle for the cat adoption clinic I attend on a bimonthly basis. I was so preoccupied with the clinic that I'd had little time to stress over the huge catastrophe that was hanging overhead. Today, however, as I helped the children of the community with their robes and songbooks, I felt the weight of what the arrest of Father Kilian could do to the people I grew up with and loved like family.

Finn wanted to keep the whole thing a secret for another couple of days. Mrs. Trexler had no family on the island to worry about her, and as far as her neighbors knew she was away on an unplanned trip, a rumor that had been started by Cody at Finn's request. Father Kilian had been asked to continue with regularly scheduled services, and Cody, Danny, Tara, and I had been sworn to secrecy until further notice.

"I have butterflies in my stomach," I whispered to Cody as the kids began lining up to enter the main body of the church, where most of the town's residents were waiting.

"The kids will be fine," Cody assured me.

"I'm not worried about the kids. It just seems so weird to carry on with our usual routine after what's happened."

"Yeah, it is a little odd. Finn knows what he's doing. The situation is volatile, and he doesn't want to create a panic until he knows what's really going on. If he can find the killer before announcing Mrs.

Trexler's death he won't have to bring Father Kilian into it at all."

"I don't know how Father Kilian is going to be able to perform mass as if nothing has happened."

"Father Kilian is a strong man with a strong faith. I believe him capable of doing whatever he feels is the right thing to do," Cody reassured me. "How about we help him out with some roof-raising music?"

"Is everything okay?" Sister Mary asked.

Although St. Patrick's wielded a lot of power in our small community, the staff consisted of one priest, Father Kilian, one nun, Sister Mary, and Ms. Winters, the housekeeper. Father Kilian took care of most of the church business, while Sister Mary ran the children's program.

"Everything is fine," Cody answered the red-haired woman with deep blue eyes and an angelic smile. "Cait is just a little nervous about her debut as choir director, so I'm giving her a pep talk."

"Don't worry." Sister Mary smiled. "The kids are going to sing with voices from heaven."

One of the things I liked the most about Sister Mary was that she was always positive and optimistic, and she always had a serene look on her face that communicated the fact that she, more than most, was able to go with the flow and not stress the small stuff. I don't think I could ever remember her being upset or agitated. The woman had a way of sharing her positive energy so that you immediately felt less stressed just by being in her presence.

"Thank you." I let out a deep breath and felt myself begin to unwind. "I'm sure they will."

Sister Mary was correct; once mass began I realized I'd worried for nothing. Father Kilian seemed confident and relaxed and gave a wonderful sermon on fidelity. The choir was energetic and on key, and I couldn't picture a single person suspecting that just two days before a brutal murder had occurred in the very building where the community had come to worship.

After mass I headed over to my mother's, as I do every Sunday. I've found that in the midst of uncertainty there are certain things I can count on in life. While the list is short, Sunday dinner at Mom's remains firmly on top. While the previous Sunday the Hart family dinner had included only Mom, my sixteen-year-old sister Cassidy, and me, this week there were going to be nine of us: Mom, Cassidy, my oldest brother Aiden, Aunt Maggie and Marley, Danny, Tara, Cody, and me.

Upon arriving at the large two-story home where I was raised, I headed toward the kitchen to help with preparations for the communal meal. The entire house smelled wonderful. If I had to guess, I'd say we were having Italian. The scents of garlic and tomato filled the air and I was certain fresh ground sausage lingered from an earlier browning.

I paused to check my appearance in the mirror over the dining hutch as I opened the top right drawer and picked out an apron. I glanced at the photos of my family on the hutch as I tied the apron around my waist. I come from a large family with deep roots on the island. My great-great-grandfather, Bernard Hart, had been one of the twelve men who had originally come over from Ireland and settled on the island. Bernard had been a fisherman who'd worked his entire life to build a fishing empire to hand down to the generations who would come after him. At one time there had been many members of the Hart family living on the island and working in the fishing industry, but things had changed in recent years and most of the Hart aunts and uncles had moved on.

I picked up a photo taken of my siblings and me five years earlier. My dad was still alive then, and my older sister Siobhan still lived on the island. I remember this six-bedroom house being filled with both laughter and arguing as the five Hart siblings tried to make their own way. My oldest brother Aiden inherited my father's fishing business when he died. It's harder to make a living in the fishing industry now than it used to be, and Aiden spends most of every summer in Alaska, where the fish are still plentiful.

Siobhan doesn't get along with my mother all that well, and she hasn't come home much since Dad died. Danny was the third Hart child to be born and now runs the *Hart of the Sea* whale watching charters out of the harbor in Pelican Bay.

The baby of the family is my little sister Cassidy. She's younger than me by ten years and has lived alone in the house with my mother since my dad died. Sometimes I feel bad for her. I know that the oftentimes quiet childhood she has experienced is a lot different from the noisy childhood my siblings and I enjoyed.

I set the photo down and continued on to the kitchen. There were five women there preparing the afternoon meal. My mom was talking to Maggie and Marley, while Tara was helping Cassie make a cake. I lingered in the doorway, trying to pick up the trend of the conversation going on around me.

"I heard there's going to be an emergency council meeting on Tuesday to discuss the special election," Mom said to Aunt Maggie, who was dicing tomatoes for the salad.

"That's what I've been told. I'm hoping that with everything that's happened the council will realize that trying to rush through a special election just to appease Bill Powell is an unwise thing to do."

"It seems like the remaining council members are simply reacting to the pressure of the moment without taking the time to really stop to think things through," Marley agreed.

For those of you who may not know the history, the island council is made up of five elected officials who make important decisions regarding the future of the island. The council members have always been leaders in the community who, once elected, tended to remain in place until they either died or moved away. It's been years since a council seat has been up for grabs. A few months ago one of the members, Gary Pixley, announced his plan to retire at the end of his current term, and an election to fill his seat had been scheduled for November.

Aunt Maggie and three other longtime residents had filed paperwork indicating their intention to run for the open seat. Things got complicated, though, when one of the members of the council was murdered. As a result, a special election to fill his seat had been announced. At that point Gary had decided to retire early, leaving the residents of the island four candidates and two seats to fill.

Once the wheels had been put into motion for this very hurried election, another man, Rick Nesbit, had pointed out that the deadline for nominees for the November election had not yet passed. He felt that the special election shouldn't be limited to those who had filed early; there might be other members of the community who'd intended to run but just hadn't gotten around to filing the paperwork. Rick was insisting that the special election be postponed until all interested parties had been given the opportunity both to file and campaign for both positions.

While Rick wasn't wrong, there were other points of view, including that of Bill Powell, a businessman from the mainland, whose condominium development project was supposed to be voted on in June. Bill continued to insist that the vote regarding his project take place sooner rather than later. The way it now stood, the council was split on the condo development, so a vote without a fifth member would be pointless. Although I hated to see the election hurried, Bill had a lot of money invested in the project and seemed to have a legitimate gripe.

Which brought us back to the discussion in my mother's kitchen as the women cooked, while the men watched the ball game on television.

"I know that with Keith's death and Gary's resignation things have come to a screeching halt, but I also believe it will bring discord to the island if this very sensitive election isn't handled properly," Maggie insisted.

"Besides, you need an opportunity to get your strength back," Marley added.

While we still didn't know who had been poisoning Maggie, it was my opinion that the addition of arsenic to her tea had been an attempt to remove her from contention in the election. Prior to getting sick, Maggie, an opponent of the condo project, had been considered to be a front runner among the pool of eligible candidates. Since her illness she had been unable to campaign or even meet her usual community obligations.

"I'll be fine," Maggie insisted. "There's no cause to worry about me, but with two seats to fill, the outcome of the vote on Bill Powell's development will most surely be decided by the views of those who are elected. The project is such a volatile subject anyway. I'd hate to see a hurry-up approach end in a decision that could lead to a political nightmare."

My mom had been smiling at me while I was catching you up, so I knew she saw me there, but so far she hadn't asked me to do anything to help with dinner. I really was much too distracted to chop veggies or butter bread, so I decided to wander into the living room. Not that I'm not as concerned as anyone about what might become of our island as a result of the vote, but I've heard it all before, and right now I was a lot more focused on Mrs. Trexler's death than on Bill Powell's condo project. Of course Cody, Tara, Danny, and I had promised Finn we wouldn't discuss the matter with anyone, not even my family, so unless I could pull aside one of the other three I had no one with whom to discuss the situation.

I continued into the den, where Danny and Aiden were arguing over the playoff situation. I love both of my brothers and I know they love each other, but as far back as I can remember they've never agreed on anything, whether it be big or small. Aiden is a conservative who very much embodies the values you'll find in the blue-collar environment of Harthaven, where hard work, family, church, and tradition are the cornerstones of everyday life. Danny has an eye to the future. He appears to embrace the more relaxed lifestyle that can be found in Pelican Bay, where the emphasis is on personal enrichment, spiritual freedom, and economic prosperity.

Although my brothers are very different, I love them both very much. They each have wonderful qualities that I'm lucky to have in my life. Danny is fun and spontaneous and much more of a friend, but if you're ever in a bad situation and really need someone to come through for you, Aiden is the brother you want at your side.

I tried to catch Cody's eye. Normally he wouldn't have been my first choice of chatting partner, but I had a few ideas to bounce off someone and he seemed to be the easiest to free up at that particular time.

"Mom needs milk, so I'm going to walk down to the corner market. Would you like to come?" I asked.

Cody shrugged. "Sure, I'll come." He got up and followed me out the front door.

"Is your mom really out of milk?" Cody asked once we had started down the hedge-lined sidewalk.

"I don't know." I stopped to pick a flower from the vine of tiny yellow roses that hugged the white picket fence lining my mother's property. "Probably not. I just needed an excuse to go to the market."

"So you wanted to get me alone," Cody teased.

"Don't flatter yourself," I said as I tucked the rose into my dark hair. "I just wanted to talk about that thing we aren't supposed to talk about and you seemed the least involved. I'm sorry if you're missing the game."

Cody shrugged. "I could use some fresh air, and the game wasn't all that exciting. So what's on your mind?"

Cody's bright blue shirt matched his eyes perfectly, and for a moment I forgot why I had initiated the ruse in the first place. I looked out toward the sea, which was visible in the distance, and refocused my mind.

"I can't help thinking about Mrs. Trexler. I've been going over every possible scenario in my mind," I began. "There's just something really off about this whole thing."

"Off how?" Cody asked.

"For one thing, why was Mrs. Trexler at the church at that time of the day on a Friday? Regular confession is held on Saturday mornings. What was so important that she couldn't wait a few hours?"

"It seemed pretty apparent to me that whatever was on her mind was a volatile subject."

"Yeah, I guess, but how did she get there? It's not like she gets around all that easily. She hasn't driven since Finn pulled her driver's license. I didn't see a car waiting for her, so she must have been dropped off. And if she was dropped off she'd most likely arranged for a ride home. Why hasn't whoever was supposed to drive her home come forward to say that she's missing?"

"You *have* been thinking about this."

"A lot," I confirmed. "I just don't feel like things are adding up. Have you considered the timeline? We saw Father Kilian and Mrs. Trexler arguing. Then we went into the choir room, where we remained for maybe twenty minutes. When we came back Mrs. Trexler was dead and Father Kilian was in his home.

It's either convenient or unfortunate that Sister Mary was away that day and so unable to act as an alibi for Father Kilian. I don't want to believe that he would do such a thing, but I have to ask myself what the likelihood is that anyone other than him could possibly have killed Mrs. Trexler."

Cody stopped walking and looked at me. The sun settled on my bare shoulders, filling my body with a relaxing warmth as he stared into my eyes. "Do you think he did it? Is that what all this speculation is about?"

I couldn't help but flinch. It felt so wrong even to consider the possibility. "I don't want to think he did it. He's been the foundation on which this community has stood since before I was born. He doesn't seem like an evil man. I can't imagine what could have occurred for him to have acted in violence, but I'm also having a heck of a time coming up with an alternative explanation."

Cody scrunched his nose and then offered a concept. "How about this: What if there was already someone in the church when Father Kilian and Mrs. Trexler arrived?"

"Like who?" I asked.

"I don't know. Let's just assume that the person was there for a reason unrelated to Mrs. Trexler and Father Kilian's argument. Maybe it was a homeless person there for shelter, or maybe it was someone who was there to steal something. Father Kilian and Mrs. Trexler came in and this person hid. After Father Kilian left the person came out of hiding, assuming both parties had left. Mrs. Trexler saw him and he killed her."

I frowned. "Do you really think that's what happened?"

"No. Probably not. But this scenario does demonstrate that there's a possible explanation that leaves Father Kilian not guilty. If there's one alternate scenario there have to be others. My point is that at this time all we can do is believe what we feel to be true and continue to search for what really happened. In your heart, do you believe Father Kilian could have done this?"

"No, I don't."

"Then trust that. We'll figure things out."

Cody took my hand and we continued down the sidewalk. Suddenly I remembered why I had always loved him. It wasn't his shaggy brown hair or deep blue eyes. It wasn't even his amazing physique or adorable dimple. It was because, more than anyone I knew, he trusted his instincts, believed in his ability to solve any problem, and always had faith that things would work out the way they were supposed to.

Chapter 3

Monday, June 1

I swatted at the feather in my face. At least it felt like a feather. I was still asleep, but I could feel myself being slowly pulled toward consciousness by something brushing the skin on my cheek. As I struggled toward wakefulness, I realized that the offending object was not a feather but a paw. A white furry paw.

"Come on, Alice. I had a late night. Just a few more minutes."

Alice climbed onto my chest, curled up in a ball, and started to purr.

"I suppose you're hungry."

The fur ball on my chest nuzzled her head under my chin. If I wasn't awake before I would be now, with her loud motor so close to my ear.

I reached up and scratched the furry cat under the chin. She really was soft and fluffy. And affectionate. Given the fact that she wore a collar with her name on it, I had to assume she wasn't a stray. I really should be putting more effort into finding her family. Chances were they were missing her.

I sat up and slipped on my knee-high slippers, as well as the oversize sweatshirt that hung down to my knees that I used for a robe. I let Max out to do his morning business while I fed Alice and started the coffee. By the time Max returned, damp and sandy from his romp on the beach in front of my cabin,

Alice was done eating, so I fed Max and headed into the kitchen to make my own eggs and toast.

I had just cracked the eggs into a frying pan when I heard a crash. I turned to see that Alice had jumped up onto the counter near the door and knocked my keys, wallet, and a flyer from the church onto the floor. It had been late when I'd gotten home the previous evening, so I'd just left everything on the counter rather than putting it away.

I picked everything up and set it on the table before turning to butter my toast. I'd barely managed one slice when Alice knocked everything to the floor again.

"Alice, quit it," I admonished the playful feline.

She let out a loud meow and lay down on the flyer announcing the events the church would be sponsoring for Founders Day.

"You want that stuff to be on the floor, it can be on the floor. I'm going to eat breakfast before it gets cold."

Alice stood up and walked around the room. I was just sitting back down at the table when she jumped up onto the fireplace mantel and knocked off one of the photos displayed there. I cringed as a loud crashing sound informed me that the glass of the frame had shattered upon impact with the wood floor.

"Okay; that's it." I got up and headed for the broom closet. "I'm pretty sure I've never met a pushier cat. I got up early to feed you. I cleaned your litter box. You're all set, so chill while I eat my breakfast in peace and quiet. Is that really too much to ask?"

Alice jumped up onto the table and rolled over onto her back in a show of surrender. I quickly swept up the glass shards and was about to go for the mop when I noticed which photo Alice had knocked down. It was one of Father Kilian, holding me on the day I was baptized. I looked at the picture and felt a tug at my heart strings. There was no way this kind man was guilty of murder. I didn't know how I could have suspected him.

"I suppose I should go talk to him," I said aloud. "Maybe I can help."

Alice jumped off the table and headed for the front door.

"I'm going to eat my eggs and shower and dress first. I'm afraid you'll need to stay here with Max. Animals aren't allowed in the church."

The eggs were so cold by this time that they weren't even worth choking down, so I headed to the shower, thinking about the approach I would take with the man who had been such an important part of my family and my community for so many years. I let the warm water flow over my head and down my back as I again tried to make sense of the events of Friday evening.

Cody and I had witnessed Father Kilian and Mrs. Trexler arguing from the hallway. We hadn't actually entered the main body of the church, so there could have been someone else inside we hadn't been aware of. Of course, Father Kilian would most likely have been aware of other parishioners who might have been there, and as far as I knew he hadn't said anything to Finn about other people on the premises.

After I got out of the shower I dressed in a bright-colored sundress and white sandals and brushed out my long, thick hair and pulled it into a clip. I checked with Maggie to confirm that she didn't need me to tend to the cats in the sanctuary, then headed into town. By the time I arrived at the church Father Kilian was already out in his flower garden, clipping the dead buds from the bushes.

"Morning, Father," I greeted him as I walked up.

"Caitlin, I'm so glad you stopped by. I've needed to speak to you, but I'm afraid an opportunity hasn't presented itself."

"I was in Seattle on Saturday and with my family yesterday," I confirmed.

"Please come into the house. I'll make us some tea."

I followed Father Kilian into his small, cozy house, wondering if he wanted to speak to me about the same thing I'd come to discuss with him.

"Can I get you something?" Ms. Winters asked as we walked in through the front door.

"Caitlin and I were planning to have some tea," Father Kilian said.

"I'll fetch it right away."

Father Kilian showed me down the hall to a small study, indicating that I should take a seat on a wingback chair near the fireplace. Then he sat down in the chair opposite the small table where Ms. Winters had set the tea service.

Ms. Winters must have seen me speaking to Father Kilian outside and started the tea. There was no way she could have had it ready that fast otherwise. Ms. Winters was known throughout the community for her efficiency. Father Kilian kept the island on track, and Ms. Winters kept Father Kilian on track.

I picked up my cup and politely sipped the surprisingly delicious brew while I waited for him to speak.

"I have something to tell you," he began. "To be honest, I'm not certain we should even be having this conversation. I've struggled with my decision for the past couple of days. As I worked in the garden this morning, I'd pretty much decided to speak to you if the opportunity presented itself, and within minutes of making my decision you came walking up."

"Alice sent me."

"Alice?"

"Never mind. What did you want to talk about?"

"I wanted to speak to you about the events of Friday evening. You'll need to bear with me as I work through exactly what I'm about to say."

I waited in silence.

"Mrs. Trexler came to see me on Friday in the late afternoon. She insisted that she needed to make an emergency confession, even though it was after-hours. She seemed extremely distraught, so I agreed to do as she requested. Even though the confessional is always a confidential place to discuss that which is troubling anyone who enters, Mrs. Trexler specifically asked for my assurance that I wouldn't repeat anything she shared with me. Despite the fact that she's passed, I still feel bound to honor the sanctity of the confessional. I told Finn as much when I spoke with him."

I frowned. I wasn't sure where this was going, but I decided to let Father Kilian set the pace for our conversation. I could see the man was in a great deal of distress and the last thing I wanted to do was to add to that.

"I want to assure you that I didn't kill Mrs. Trexler."

"Oh, of course not." I leaned forward and placed one of my hands over his. "I never thought you did. Well, not really."

"If you had suspected me I would understand. Sometimes extreme circumstances can cause us to doubt what we believe to be true. I've known you your whole life, but for a brief moment I thought maybe *you* might have done it."

"Me? Why would I kill Mrs. Trexler?"

"It appeared you had the motive to do so."

"Motive? What motive? I liked the woman. I visited her twice a week and made sure her pantry was stocked and that she had homemade meals for her freezer."

"Your generosity in the community is widely known and respected. That's why once I thought about it some more I realized you wouldn't act with violence, even if you had reason to do so."

"Again I have to ask: what reason?"

"Mrs. Trexler and I were arguing because she'd confessed something to me that I felt she needed to confess to another person as well. She refused to do so, even though that person was harmed by her actions. I tried to convince her to do the right thing, but the more I argued my point, the more stubbornly she refused to even consider doing so. I decided I was allowing my emotions to get the better of me, so I excused myself to take a moment to deal with my anger, which I realized wasn't appropriate in the church. I left Mrs. Trexler in the church, requesting that she pray about the situation while I was out of the room. I asked that she come to find me when she was ready to continue our discussion. The next thing I knew, Cody was at my door to inform me that the woman was dead. I hadn't even known that you and Cody were in the church."

"We came in when you were arguing. We couldn't hear what was being said, but it looked fairly intense."

"Yes." Father Kilian sighed. "I'm afraid the argument got the better of both of us. I'm sure Finn has asked you this already, but did you see anyone else in or around the building that night?"

"No. Cody and I came in, saw you arguing, and discreetly headed to the choir room. We were in there no more than twenty minutes. We got the music we'd come for and headed out. We noticed the lights on in the church but didn't see anyone, so I went in to turn them off. That's when I discovered Mrs. Trexler's body. Cody called 911, Finn arrived, and I guess you know the rest."

Father Kilian sat back in his chair. His blue eyes, faded with age, looked tired and bloodshot. If I had to guess I'd say he hadn't slept since the incident. He ran a hand through his gray hair as he tried to make up his mind about something. I imagine it would be difficult to be in his shoes. On one hand, he'd been sworn to secrecy, but on the other, he knew something he probably wished he hadn't been burdened with.

I decided to start working through what I did know to see if I could figure out what it was Father Kilian wanted to share but felt obligated not to. "It makes sense that Mrs. Trexler might have been killed because of whatever it was she confessed to you. You thought I might have been the one to do it when you realized I was in the building, but Mrs. Trexler has never done anything to harm me, so what motive would I have?"

"I believed you might have acted to protect someone you love."

"Someone I love? I guess if I was going to go all Rambo on someone the threat to a loved one would be a reason to do so, but I really can't see…" I paused as the truth suddenly set in. "The tea. Mrs. Trexler poisoned Maggie's tea."

Father Kilian didn't say anything, but I could see by the look on his fact that I was right.

"But why? Mrs. Trexler liked Maggie. At least I thought she did. Why would she want to make her sick?"

"To be honest, I don't actually know that Mrs. Trexler tampered with the tea. She did seem to know who had done the tampering, though, and for whatever reason she refused to turn that person in. I've thought about this a lot in the past few days, and the only explanation I can come up with is that Mrs. Trexler had information about another resident she knew well, liked, and respected. I tried to explain to her that confessing to me wasn't enough, but she refused to say who she was covering for."

"If Maggie had drunk more of the tea, or if the amount of arsenic added to it had been miscalculated, she might have died."

"I know."

I felt a rush of anger. No wonder Father Kilian had been so mad.

"I can't believe she was protecting this person. Do you think the person she was protecting knew she was developing a conscience and killed her to keep her quiet?"

"I wish I knew."

Chapter 4

By the time I arrived at Coffee Cat Books the place was overrun with men taking down walls and hauling away debris. If Tara had her way about it, the building would be remodeled before summer's end, and I was starting to become almost as excited as her about the project. Not only would it allow me to spend my days with three of my favorite things— coffee, cats, and books—but it would allow me to carve out my own source of income, rather than depending on part-time work provided by Maggie or Danny.

"Wow, you've already gotten a lot done," I commented when I walked into the building, stepping over a toolbox near the entrance. Tara was holding a rolled-up blueprint and speaking to a man in paint-covered overalls.

"You'll need to wear a hard hat when the men are working." Tara handed me a yellow one. "How come you're so late?"

"I was talking to Father Kilian," I answered as the man Tara had been talking to walked away.

"How is he today? He looked so tired yesterday. I don't think he's been sleeping well."

"I'm sure he hasn't. I'll explain everything later, but I'm really on my way to speak to Finn. I knew I was supposed to help out today, so I decided to stop by to let you know something was up."

"Something's up?"

"Yeah, but I can't talk about it here. It's still early and I shouldn't be long. I'll come back to help when

I'm done. Do you want me to bring you back some lunch or something?"

"Yeah, that would be nice."

I looked around the room. "Where are Danny and Cody? I thought they were going to help."

"Danny ended up with a last-minute whale watching charter and Cody is over at Mr. Parsons's. He had a fall, and Cody wanted to check in with him to make sure he was okay."

"I hadn't heard. Was it a serious fall?" I asked.

Tara shrugged. "I'm not sure. Cody got the call shortly after he arrived. I haven't heard from him since."

"Okay, then, I'll head over to speak to Finn and then go to check on Mr. Parsons. I'll pick us up some lunch and be back after that."

"I'll be here." Tara smiled as she waved at one of the men carrying lumber and redirected their path.

I decided to call Cody before heading over to see Finn. Mr. Parsons wasn't a young man and a fall at his age could result in a serious injury. Cody informed me that he'd taken Mr. Parsons to the clinic for an x-ray and would call me when he got the results. We both hoped the elderly man hadn't broken anything, but Cody said he seemed to be in quite a lot of pain.

Finn's office was located on Second Street, one block up from Main. It occupied the middle space in a larger building that had been subdivided to create five smaller offices from the original space, which had at one time been occupied by a family who built midsize fishing boats. It really isn't so much an office as a small space wedged between the old newspaper, which had recently shut down, and the post office.

Sometimes I wonder why Finn even bothers to open the closet-sized office every day. He spends very little time there, but I guess it gives him the opportunity to meet with folks who want to stop in to chat, so he holds office hours each morning.

"Just the woman I wanted to see," Finn greeted me the moment I walked through the door.

"Really? Why?"

"I think I might have a lead on Maggie's poisoning."

"Mrs. Trexler either did it or knows who did it and was covering for them."

"What? That wasn't what I was going to say. Why would Mrs. Trexler poison Maggie?"

I filled Finn in on my conversation with Father Kilian.

"I find it hard to believe that Mrs. Trexler would do such a thing." Finn shook his head in disbelief. "She was my third-grade teacher."

"I know. Mine too."

"My instinct tells me there's more going on than there seems," Finn said. "This whole thing just isn't adding up. It makes no sense that Mrs. Trexler would poison Maggie or protect the person who did if she wasn't directly involved. And it definitely makes no sense that Father Kilian would kill Mrs. Trexler, although I don't have any other suspects at the moment."

"Maybe we should look around Mrs. Trexler's house to see if we can turn up anything. If she was in any way involved in poisoning Maggie's tea we might find something that would lead us to exactly what occurred."

Finn stood up from behind his desk. "I was planning to go over there today anyway. I was just waiting to get the go ahead from the main office."

"I'm going with you," I stated.

"I figured."

I'd left my car at the old cannery and walked over to Finn's office, so I rode with him in his squad car over to Mrs. Trexler's house. When we arrived Alice was sitting on the front porch as if she were waiting for us.

"Mrs. Trexler's cat?" Finn guessed.

"No. She didn't have a cat. This is Alice. She's connected to the case."

"Connected to the case? How?" Finn asked.

"I'm not sure yet; she showed up just after Mrs. Trexler's murder and seems to have strong opinions as to what should be done next. I say we let her inside and see where she leads us."

"You think we should follow the cat?"

I nodded.

Finn stared at me, one eyebrow raised in question.

"What can it hurt? It's not like we know where to look, or even what we're looking for."

Finn shrugged. He picked the lock and opened the door. Alice trotted in and headed down the hallway toward the back.

The house was neat and tidy. Finn focused on the living room, while I followed Alice down the hall to Mrs. Trexler's bedroom. The cat trotted over to the four-shelf bookcase that stood in one corner. She reached out a paw and pulled one of the books off the shelf. It was a small book, barely larger than a piece of bread. I picked it up and saw it was a journal of some sort, although the book was locked. I looked behind me to see that Finn was still rummaging around in the front of the house. I'm not sure why I made the split-second decision to hide the book from him, but I found myself slipping it into the front pocket of my sweatshirt.

Finn walked into the bedroom behind me just as I was shifting the small book so the bulge wouldn't be obvious.

"Nothing in the front of the house. Anything in here?" he asked me.

"I haven't found anything so far," I lied.

Finn looked at Alice. "Well? If you're here to lead us to a clue, then lead away."

Alice turned around and left the bedroom. She trotted over to a small table near the front door and knocked a stack of mail to the floor. Finn leaned over and picked it up. He frowned. "It looks like a bank statement and a letter from Orson Cobalter."

Orson used to operate the only newspaper on Madrona Island. He'd had a heart attack the previous winter and closed down the paper in order to go live with his children in Florida. The small local paper was for sale, but so far no one had bought it.

"What does the letter say?" I asked.

Finn looked in the envelope. "It's empty. Mrs. Trexler must have taken the letter but left the envelope here in the pile. Other than the bank statement the rest is junk mail." Finn slipped the envelope and the bank statement into his shirt pocket. "Guess it wouldn't hurt to try to contact Orson, and to talk to the folks at the bank just in case your cat is on to something."

"Yeah, couldn't hurt."

"I heard Camden Bradford quit his job at the bank in order to take care of his sister," Finn added.

"Yeah, she's taking the whole thing really hard and Cam wanted to be there for her. He's talking about taking both his mom and his sister on a long trip until this whole mess blows over."

Cam had been working for the bank on a temporary basis in order to help out his brother-in-law, who had been injured in an accident. When Cam found out that his brother-in-law was guilty of participating in a blackmail scheme, he'd helped Finn solve the case at great personal cost to his family. I hadn't liked or trusted him at first, but now that he was gone from my life I found I missed him.

"That's probably best," Finn agreed. "Do you think there's anything else to find here?"

I looked at Alice, who was lying by the front door. "No, I think that we're done here. If you wouldn't mind giving Alice and me a ride back to my car I think I'll take my feline friend home. It's a long way for her to walk twice in one day."

When I got home I called Cody, who informed me that Mr. Parsons had fractured his leg and was going to need to spend a day or two in the hospital due to his age. Cody was going to move his stuff over to Mr. Parsons's house; our mutual friend needed someone to care for Rambler while he was in the hospital and would need someone to care for him when he returned home himself. It really was nice of Cody to volunteer to take care of Mr. Parsons, but he had a huge house, so I was certain both men would be comfortable.

Cody agreed to stop by my cabin after he got settled. I was anxious to fill him in on the events of the morning and get his take on what might really be going on with Mrs. Trexler. I knew Tara planned to come over after she finished up at Coffee Cat Books so we could watch *Cooking With Cathy* together. I'd volunteered to do the prep work for the recipe we were making that night because I'd totally bailed on helping out with the remodel, as I'd promised to do.

I glanced at the clock on the wall and decided I had time to take Max for a quick run on the beach before Cody arrived. I left a note just in case he was earlier than he anticipated and then headed out the door with Max on my heels. It really was a gorgeous day. The sun was high in the sky and the ocean was a deep cobalt blue. A pair of bald eagles flew overhead as the waves lapped gently to the shore. The sun was warm on my shoulders as I settled into an easy rhythm. I took a deep breath of the clean, salty air as Max chased seagulls and splashed through the rolling surf.

I love my little corner of the world. Living on a small island isn't for everyone, mainly due to the isolation that can seem stifling, especially in the winter. A lot of my friends went away to college after high school and many never came back. I guess a part of me understands the draw of big city life, but I wouldn't trade my little cabin and deserted stretch of beach for a penthouse apartment in the finest neighborhood in the most desirable city in the world.

I stopped to watch a pair of orcas who were frolicking near where the open water met the channel, a place many of the whales liked to hang out. I knew Danny was out that day and wondered if he knew that at least one of the pods had moved from the open water, where they had been congregating during the past week. I pulled my phone out of my pocket and texted him the location of the whales. Danny was good at what he did and almost always managed to find whales for his guests to photograph and enjoy, but even tour captains like Danny had an off day every now and then.

"I'm glad the whales are back," a young girl who appeared to be twelve or thirteen, with long braids hanging down either side of her head, walked up and began petting Max.

"So am I." I smiled. "My name is Cait."

"I'm Haley. Do you live nearby?"

"In the cabin just down the beach. How about you?"

"I'm staying with my aunt for the summer. My mom is in the hospital. She's really sick and my dad can't deal with me."

"I'm so sorry." My heart bled for the child who spoke in such a matter of fact way about such a horrible situation. "It must be hard for you to be away from your family."

The girl shrugged. "Mom has been sick for a long time and Dad has been sad for a long time. My aunt sings while she does the housework and smiles at me when I come down to breakfast."

"Who is your aunt? Maybe I know her."

"Her name is Delilah."

I was pretty sure I didn't know anyone named Delilah and I knew almost everyone on the island. "Has she lived here long?" I asked.

"No. She's renting a house for the summer. She's an artist, so she's here to paint."

I stopped to pick up a shell. The cold water washed over my bare feet as I stood talking to the girl. "Are the two of you here alone?"

"Yup, it's just us."

"I'll have to come down and meet her sometime," I said as the water receded, pulling the sand from under my feet. "Where exactly do you live?"

"Up the beach on the other side of the jetty. The house is yellow. I like yellow. It's my favorite color."

"That's pretty far. Did you walk all the way down here by yourself?"

"I rode my bike to the end of the road and then walked. I wanted to see the cats, but there was no one there."

"Max and I were just about to head back. If you want to walk with us I can show you the cats. Did your aunt tell you about the sanctuary?"

"No. A lady in town did. She said you had kittens and might need someone to play with them. Dell likes me to stay out of her way when she's working, so I thought I'd try to get a job."

"You know," I said, "I've been thinking we need someone to play with the kittens. It helps to socialize them."

The girl smiled. "I would do a good job, I promise. I got all As in school and my teacher said I was a hard worker."

"How about we try you out and see how it goes?"

"Really?" The girl had the widest smiled I'd ever seen.

"Really," I confirmed.

Haley hugged me and squealed with happiness. She turned and did a line of cartwheels down the beach, with Max barking alongside her the entire time. I really hoped Haley worked out. The girl was fun and likable. It would be nice to have her energy as part of my everyday life.

It turned out Haley was wonderful with all the cats. Even the crankiest feral adults seemed to like her. I told her that if she was going to come over every day I'd need to speak to her aunt, so I gave her a ride home. Delilah was delighted that her niece would have something to keep her occupied for part of every day, so I arranged to pick her up after my exercise class the following morning.

I showered and changed into clean shorts and a tank top when I returned to the cabin. I left my feet bare as I began assembling ingredients for the pizza casserole Tara and I were making that night. Luckily, there wasn't a lot of prep work for this particular dish other than to grate cheese. I was just putting the last of the utensils I'd used into the dishwasher when Cody showed up at my door with Rambler.

"How is Mr. Parsons?" I asked as Cody slid onto one of the bar stools surrounding my kitchen counter while the dogs greeted each other and Alice headed for the stairs to the loft.

"He was in a lot of pain, but they have him on medication and he's resting comfortably now. I'm glad he called me. He wasn't even going to go to the doctor at first. In fact, it took quite a bit of convincing for me to get him to go when I showed up. He was sure it was just a sprain."

"I'm glad he called you too. It was nice of you to volunteer to stay with him."

"I'm happy to do it. I was getting tired of staying at the inn anyway. I'll be glad for the company, but

I'm sorry Mr. Parsons is in so much pain. So, fill me in on your conversation with Finn. I've been dying to hear ever since you mentioned speaking to him."

I filled Cody in on my conversation with Father Kilian, as well as my conversation with Finn. I told him about the envelope from Orson Cobalter, as well as the journal I'd found but hadn't yet had time to read. Cody hadn't heard that Orson had decided to sell the newspaper, and I was surprised to see that he was more than just a little interested in learning about the details of the sale.

"Are you considering buying the paper?" I asked.

"I might be," Cody informed me.

Cody had been a reporter for the high school newspaper when he wasn't leading the football team to victory or starring in the annual high school musical, so I guess I shouldn't have been surprised.

"So you *are* thinking about staying. On the island. Permanently?"

"I guess I am." Cody shrugged. "I came to Madrona Island to try to figure out the next phase in my life. I've really enjoyed being here and renewing old friendships. It's been fun helping out with the choir, and Mr. Parsons asked me about moving in with him on a more permanent basis."

"You're going to live with him?"

"Sort of. He'll need someone to help him on the first floor until he can get around again, but he asked if I'd be interested in living in the rooms on the third floor. He said he hasn't even been up there in years, but there were several large rooms as well as a bathroom. We'd need to share the kitchen, or I suppose I could convert one of the upstairs rooms into a kitchen, but Mr. Parsons is getting on in years and he really could use someone to look in on him, do the shopping, and prepare meals."

"I do that now."

"I know. And he appreciates it more than you know. I guess he figures that I've been living at the inn and he has this huge house that he only uses a portion of, and it might be nice to have someone around to help out and provide some company. If I decided to do it you will, of course, be welcome to come over as often as you like."

I wiped the last of the grated cheese from the counter. "It sounds like you've given this a lot of thought."

"Not really. Mr. Parsons just brought it up while we were at the hospital today. I've been thinking about staying on the island, but I wasn't sure what I would do about a job. I have quite a bit of money saved up, but I'll need a steady source of income eventually. The thought of reopening the paper is really intriguing."

"I'm pretty sure it was losing money even before Orson decided to shut it down due to his health issues," I pointed out.

"Maybe. But Orson didn't believe in providing online issues, and he didn't work the advertising the way he should have."

"How would you know? You haven't been here for ten years," I said.

"I tried to order the paper online so I could stay connected to the island, and I spoke to him about it several times. He said he would need to buy new computer equipment and it didn't seem worth it. I tried to convince him about the benefit of the expanded revenue source online issues would provide, but he was pretty set in his ways. When I noticed the building was empty I asked about it but was only told that Orson hadn't been feeling well and had gone to stay with his children. I didn't realize he wanted to sell."

I tried to decide how I felt about Cody staying on the island, reopening the newspaper, moving in with Mr. Parsons—who just happened to live next door to me—and becoming a permanent part of my everyday life. A few weeks ago I would have been horrified, but now . . . now I just felt confused.

"Do you know who's handling the sale of the property?" Cody asked.

"I'm not sure. I suppose Porter Wilson must be, but I wouldn't be surprised if Orson might be trying to sell it himself."

"I guess I'll give Orson a call to chat with him. And I'll see if I can slip in an inquiry about the letter he sent to Mrs. Trexler. So about this journal . . ."

"I haven't had a chance to read any of it yet. I'm not sure why I didn't tell Finn I was taking it. I guess it occurred to me that it could be nothing more than personal things on subjects unrelated to her involvement in Aunt Maggie's poisoning or her death. And if that was the case I didn't want her personal thoughts to become evidence."

"That makes sense. I won't mention it to Finn. If you find something important you can give it to him then. I'm going to head over to Porter Wilson's office to see if I can take a look at the building and equipment Orson is selling. I'll see if I can get current contact information for him as well. Let me know if you find anything in the journal and I'll let you know if Orson knows anything that could shed some light on things. We'll catch up tomorrow," he added as he called Rambler to his side and headed out the door.

Chapter 5

Tuesday, June 2

Every Tuesday and Thursday morning Tara and I head into town and submit ourselves to an hour of torture as we bend, grind, and sweat our way through Bitzy Biner's advanced exercise class. Personally, I really enjoy the challenge, but Tara is less enthusiastic about the torture Bitzy loves to put us through. Tara is what I like to refer to as pleasantly plump. I wouldn't go so far as to say fat, but the woman loves to eat, and until I prodded her into joining the class with me, she considered sweating and any activity that brought on that unpleasant state to be her mortal enemy.

"I'm regretting my impulse to eat the casserole we made last night for breakfast this morning." Tara groaned as we were instructed to drop to the floor for crunches.

"I thought you were going to take it with you to share with the guys working on the remodel," I reminded her. Normally, we divided up the food we made during *Cooking With Cathy* between Mr. Parsons and Mrs. Trexler, but with Mrs. Trexler's murder and Mr. Parsons's hospital stay, Tara had volunteered to take the delicious but high-calorie casserole to the construction workers who had already made a lot of headway on the new shop.

"I was going to take it to them, but then my mother called and I got tense and started nibbling.

One thing led to another, and before I knew it, half the dish was empty. I didn't even bother to heat it up or put it on a plate. I just picked at it one piece at a time. I think I'm going to puke."

Tara jumped up and ran toward the bathroom. Being the good friend that I am, I followed her. It wasn't like Tara to be so impulsive. She tends toward deliberate acts and is normally not the type to eat until she makes herself sick. I waited in the locker room until she emerged, looking slightly less green.

"What's going on?" I asked. "I know your mom makes you nuts at times, but she's two thousand miles away and not likely to interfere in your life, so what gives?"

Tara hesitated. "I don't know. I guess it's a few things. I feel like I'm under a lot of stress with everything that's going on. You know I have a tendency to eat when I'm stressed. I was doing okay until my mom informed me that she was planning to come out for a visit and was bringing my Aunt Irene. Between the remodel at the cannery, Mrs. Trexler's murder, the upcoming Founders Day event, and the whole debacle with Danny, I don't have the energy to deal with Mom *and* Aunt Irene."

"Debacle with Danny?" I asked.

Tara groaned again. "I didn't mean to say that."

"Maybe not, but you did, so what's going on with Danny?"

Tara had had a crush on Danny for years, but I knew he viewed her as nothing more than a friend. A good friend, but a friend. Tara wasn't blind to that fact, so she kept her feelings to herself, and the situation had never really been a problem before.

"Danny and I went to O'Malley's for a drink on Sunday, after you and Cody left your mom's. It was a friendly sort of drink, but then we had a second, and Danny started complaining to me that Melanie had just been using him and had never really been all that into him."

Melanie is the cocktail waitress at O'Malley's, the neighborhood pub. Danny and Melanie had dated a few times recently, and Danny seemed to be falling for her.

"I tried my best to put on my sympathetic friend hat and offer a shoulder to metaphorically cry on, even though I have no idea what he sees in her other than her fantastic figure and flawless skin," Tara continued.

"And?" I prompted.

"And we had a nice chat. We really seemed to connect, like we did when we were kids, before puberty got in the way and complicated things. We got up to leave and I noticed that he seemed a little more than mildly tipsy, so I offered to drive him home. He fell asleep in my car, and when I leaned over to wake him up he kissed me."

Yikes.

"And?" I asked.

"And I kissed him back. I should have pulled away, but I didn't. Things got intense, and then, suddenly, he opened his eyes and looked at me. I could see he was shocked. If I had to guess, I'd say he had no idea he was even kissing *me*. He was probably dreaming about Melanie and when I leaned over he must have thought he was kissing her. When he realized it was me, he bolted out of the car. I haven't spoken to him since."

"Which is the real reason he wasn't helping out with the remodel yesterday," I suggested.

"Yeah. I didn't want to get into it at that point. I'm afraid I've ruined everything. We both know I've had feelings for him since I was a kid, and we also both know he's never seen me as any more than his little sister's friend."

I paused and tried to gather my thoughts. "You know he considers you to be his friend and not just his sister's friend, but you're right. As far as I know, he's never looked at you in a romantic light."

"I don't know what I was thinking," Tara moaned "I never should have kissed him back. And I certainly shouldn't have let the kiss progress to the point that I did. I should have pulled back immediately and kidded him about sleep kissing. If I had things would be fine between us."

"And you think things aren't fine?" I asked. I could hear the class winding down in the other room.

"He didn't show up yesterday, and when I called to remind him about the changes we made to his whale watching schedule he didn't answer. I left a message, but he didn't call back. I never wanted him to know how I feel about him. Not unless I thought there was some small hope that he felt it back." Tara put her face in her hands and let out a long groan.

"The class is breaking up. Let's head out before the others come in to change," I said. "We can go back to my place and continue this discussion if you want."

"Thanks. I'm fine now, and I need to get over to the bookstore. *We* really should be on-site to monitor things and answer any questions the guys might have."

Ouch. The *we* had been delivered in a pointed tone. Tara wasn't wrong, however. I'd been letting her handle most of the work involved in the remodel.

"I'll head home, take Max for a quick run, shower, and be at the bookstore directly after that," I promised.

"Thanks. I appreciate it. I guess all of this is getting to me more than I realized. The guys are moving faster than I ever imagined. Which is awesome. But it also makes things a lot more real. We really should discuss ordering the equipment and inventory we'll need."

I hugged Tara. "Okay. I'll be there in a couple of hours. Oh, wait, no I won't."

"You won't?"

I explained about Haley and the job I had given her playing with the cats.

"That was really nice of you," Tara admitted. "I'm sure she could use a friend. Just come over to the bookstore when you can."

I took Max for a run, showered and changed, and then picked up Haley as I had arranged. She was the most enthusiastic employee I could ever have asked for. Maggie came out to give me a message before heading into town, so I was able to introduce them. After a bit of discussion it was decided that when Haley was finished with the cats I would drop her off at the Bait and Stitch, where she would help Maggie with some projects she'd been meaning to get to. Haley was thrilled to have the attention of the older woman, and Delilah was thrilled to have someone to keep her niece occupied. It turned out that she had a big show coming up in the fall that she needed to prepare for and had only decided to bring Haley with her to the island at the last minute at the request of her sick sister. She felt bad that she didn't have more time to spend with the girl, but she'd already committed to providing a large number of new pieces for the show.

After dropping Haley at the Bait and Stitch and confirming with Maggie that she would take her home at the end of the day, I headed over to Coffee Cat Books as I had promised Tara. My intention was to be the best and most helpful business partner on the island. I donned my hard hat, greeted the men, and was on my way to obtain instructions from Tara when I ran into Everett Conroy, the son of the woman who lived across the street from Mrs. Trexler.

"Morning, Everett," I greeted him. "I didn't know you were back."

"I worked in Seattle over the winter, but I'm back for the summer," he explained.

"Are you staying at your mom's?" I asked. Everett and his mother, Peggy, had moved to the island three years earlier.

"For the time being. I'd like to get my own place, but I need to save some money first. I was real glad to get hired on here as a temp after my plans fell through with Mrs. Trexler."

"You had plans with Mrs. Trexler?" I asked.

"She wanted me to paint her house. I was supposed to meet with her on Saturday, but she left town with that old guy from the post office on Friday and hasn't come back yet."

"She left town with Mr. Baxter?"

Pete Baxter was the local postmaster. He'd held that position since before I was born. He was a staple in the community who knew everyone's name and, more often than not, their personal situation as well. Of course I knew Mrs. Trexler wasn't actually out of town, but Everett seemed certain she was.

"Why do you think she left town with Mr. Baxter?" I asked.

"She was with him at the ferry station on Friday morning," Everett informed me.

"You saw her arrive with Mr. Baxter?"

"No, I didn't actually see her get there, but I'm certain it was Mr. Baxter she was talking with just prior to boarding. I just assumed they were traveling together because it was the first ferry of the day."

"And you were waiting for the ferry as well?" I asked.

"I was there to pick up my friend from Seattle, who came over to fish for a couple of days. I was in my car, which was parked on the street near the terminal, so I doubt either Mrs. Trexler or Mr. Baxter saw me. I was going to say hi, but they seemed to be having a serious conversation so I stayed put."

Pete Baxter was a lifelong resident of Madrona Island, who'd worked at the post office most of his adult life. He was a nosy sort who tended to look through everyone's mail before placing it in the post office boxes the island residents used to receive their mail. He never actually opened anyone's mail as far as I knew, but he did tend to make up stories based on what he *had* seen. Last winter when one of the women in the quilting circle began receiving mail from a male sender, Mr. Baxter suggested to those who would listen that she was stepping out on her husband. The reality was that the letters were from a nephew who was working through some issues with the woman's sister.

"Had you noticed Mr. Baxter or anyone else visiting Mrs. Trexler lately?" I asked.

Everett thought about it. "She seemed to have quite a few visitors. I saw you come by a couple of times a week, and Irma Farmer and Mrs. Tillman have both been around quite a bit."

Irma Farmer was a member of the quilting circle that met several times a week at the Bait and Stitch. She was also Mayor Bradley's next door neighbor, and was often in possession of juicy pieces of gossip before anyone else. Patience Tillman was another member of the quilting circle and the head of the senior women's group. Both of them were close to Mrs. Trexler's age and had lived on the island for years, so it wasn't odd that they would be by to visit.

"I don't suppose you know when Mrs. Trexler might be back?" Everett asked. "I'd still like to talk to her about painting her house."

"No," I lied. "I'm not sure when she's planning to return."

After I finished speaking to Everett I went in search of Tara. I know I'd promised to help her that day, but now I really wanted to head over to the post office to talk to Mr. Baxter. If he'd been speaking to Mrs. Trexler the day she died maybe she'd shared with him what was on her mind.

"Oh good, you're here," Tara said when I joined her in the area we planned to use as the coffee bar. "I've just been informed that the wall we want to add behind the bar will need to be either six feet to the left or to the right of where we discussed due to the limitation of the existing supports. One space is going to be larger than planned and one is going to be smaller."

I was surprised Tara was even asking my opinion. If I knew her, she'd already analyzed the situation and come to a conclusion as to what should be done. I could see she was really trying to make me feel part of our new venture, and I appreciated her effort, although it made me feel worse for bailing on her.

"What do you think we should do?" I asked.

"I've been looking at the plans since I was informed of the issue, and it seems to make the most sense to increase the square footage of the bookstore and decrease the square footage of the cat lounge. If we eliminate the cubicles we planned to build and just place tables under the windows that overlook the harbor I don't think we'll lose much seating area. I know the cubicles were your idea, so I didn't want to nix them without speaking to you about it."

I shrugged. "I think your plan makes the most sense. After I thought about it I realized that if people wanted to read or study in solitude they could stay home or go to the library."

"Good." Tara let out a breath. "I think adding additional space to the bookstore will allow us to carry reading-related gifts as well as books."

"I was thinking about heading out to do some errands," I began.

"But you just got here," Tara argued.

"I know. And I want to help. It's just that I got a lead on that thing we aren't supposed to talk about. I thought I'd check it out and then come right back."

Tara sighed. "Oh, all right. Can you bring me back a smoothie? I don't think my stomach is up to real food quite yet, but after my incident at the class this morning I find that I'm actually hungry."

"One smoothie coming right up. Strawberry?"

"Blackberry, if they have it. And Cait, don't forget to come back."

"I won't," I promised. "You won't even know I'm gone."

The distance between Coffee Cat Books and the post office wasn't all that far, so I decided to walk. It was a beautiful day, and if there's one thing I've learned from living my entire life in the Pacific Northwest it's that you have to embrace sunny days when they come your way. I love living on the island, but we do tend to get more fog and rain than I would prefer. Still, the weather is mild and the scenery exceptional.

The building where Coffee Cat Books would be housed is on the wharf that at one point served the fishing boats dropping off their day's catch but has since been modified to accommodate the ferry. After you leave the wharf you pass the row of touristy type shops and restaurants that have sprung up in recent years to accommodate the foot traffic generated by the ferry.

I waved to Banjo through the open door of Ship Wreck, an eclectic shop that sells a little bit of everything. Banjo and Summer are a hippie couple in their late sixties who moved to the island a little more than a year ago after deciding that it was finally time to settle down. They live in a shack just down the beach from Mr. Parsons's house. I'm not certain where Banjo and Summer are from originally, but I will say that they seem to have done an admirable job of traveling to most of the countries in the world.

They're the type of people who like to live life on their own terms. They open their shop when they feel like it, spend countless hours every week watching old soap opera reruns with Mr. Parsons, and, in spite of the fact that they don't seem to lack financial resources, live in a shack that is devoid of most modern conveniences.

After I passed Ship Wreck, I stopped to say hi to Bella and Tansy. I hadn't had much of a chance to speak to them since Friday and I wanted to assure them that Alice had arrived as predicted. I expressed my concern that the cat might belong to someone, considering the fact that she wore a collar with her name on it, but they assured me that she would find her way home when she was finished doing whatever it was she was in my life to do.

The storefront next to Herbalities, Bella and Tansy's shop, is a sushi restaurant named Off the Hook, and next to that is Maggie's store, the Bait and Stitch. There are a handful of T-shirt shops and local craft outlets, along with several sandwich shops and seafood restaurants between the Bait and Stitch and Harbor Boulevard, the side road that lead to the small strip mall on Second Street.

As I rounded the corner of Main and Harbor I noticed a group of people had gathered in front of the Driftwood Café, which was located on the corner of Harbor and Second. As I neared the popular coffee shop, I could see the restaurant was deserted. There was a sign on the door announcing that the business would be closed for a few days, reopening the following weekend.

"That's odd," I said aloud to no one in particular.

"I was in yesterday and no one said anything about being closed," a woman in a purple blouse commented.

"I had my mouth all set on one of Ernie's meatball subs," a man in a red hat complained.

I continued past the crowd and made my way down the street to the post office. Luckily, the lobby was empty. I rang the bell on the counter and Mr. Baxter emerged from the back room, where the post office boxes were loaded.

"Mornin', Cait. What can I do for you?"

"I noticed the café is closed. Any idea why?" I asked.

"I can't say for certain, but I know Ernie's dad has been in the hospital. I'd say he must have taken a turn for the worse."

That made sense. Ernie wasn't a young man, so I figured his dad had to be in his eighties at least.

"The main reason I'm here is to ask about Mrs. Trexler."

"What about her?" Mr. Baxter asked.

"I ran into Everett Conroy, and he mentioned that he saw you talking to her on Friday morning. I haven't heard from her since," I lied. "I wondered if she mentioned where she was going."

"I don't think she went anywhere," Mr. Baxter said. "I was waiting for the ferry to pick up the mail, like I do every morning. A blue sedan pulled up and Mrs. Trexler got out. The car pulled away and she joined me in the boarding area. I asked if she was heading off the island for the day and she said she was just there to pick up a package. When the ferry arrived she boarded briefly, and by the time I'd loaded the mail into my truck she'd emerged with a package in her hand and the sedan that had dropped her off picked her up."

I frowned. This whole thing was getting stranger and stranger.

"She didn't mention what she was picking up?" I asked.

"Nope."

"And you don't know who delivered the package?"

"She didn't say and I didn't ask."

"Okay. Thanks for the information." I turned toward the door. "You said you meet the ferry every day to pick up the mail?"

"Every weekday. It's part of my job."

"Have you seen Mrs. Trexler picking up any other packages recently?"

Mr. Baxter thought about it. "No, I can't say that I have. 'Course I always meet the first ferry of the day. Not a lot of people around that early."

"Yeah, I guess not. Okay, thanks."

I left the building and returned to the sunny sidewalk. The crowd that had gathered had dispersed. I imagined someone had come along to explain Ernie's absence to the satisfaction of those gathered. As I walked past the empty newspaper office I noticed that the door was ajar. I looked through the front window but didn't see anyone, so I headed inside.

"Hello?" I called.

"In the back," a voice that sounded an awful lot like Cody's answered.

"Cait, what a surprise," he said when I entered the press room. "How'd you know I'd be here?"

"I didn't. I was at the post office and noticed the door was unlocked. What are *you* doing here?"

"Just checking things out. I had a telephone conversation with Orson and I find I'm even more interested in buying the newspaper than I was before. I think there's a lot of potential for a publication like this."

I looked at the old equipment and the ink-stained floor and wondered what Cody saw in it. Something had caused a sparkle in his eye and a smile on his lips, but I didn't see a single thing that looked all that impressive. The walls, which had at one point been white, were almost black with stains, and the grease in the pit covered the floor completely.

"You're really serious about this?" I asked.

"I really am."

"Have you settled in at Mr. Parsons's?"

"I moved over yesterday. I talked to him this morning; the doctor agreed to let him come home tomorrow as long as I was going to be there to care for him."

"That's good. I'm glad he's doing better." I ran my finger over a dust-covered table. "It looks like you're going to have quite a job getting the paper up and running."

"Yeah. It's going to take some hard work and quite a bit of money. I told Orson I'd let him know for certain if I was going to buy it by the end of the week. There are some things I need to verify before I'll be ready to commit."

"Did you happen to ask him about his letter to Mrs. Trexler?" I asked.

He nodded. "He told me she'd written to him asking about an article he'd written a while back concerning the historical evolution of land ownership on the island."

"Did he know why she wanted the information?"

"He didn't say. He did tell me that he'd sent her copies of some documents he had, as well as some links to others she could obtain from the county. Did you know that all of the land on this entire island was once owned by just twelve men?"

"Yeah, the founding families. I remember once asking Maggie how she ended up owning the huge oceanfront estate where we live, and she explained that her grandfather, along with Francine Rivers's great-grandfather and Mr. Parsons's great-grandfather, had settled on the peninsula when they first arrived on the island. They divided the land between the three of them and, like most of the other landowners, they never sold it."

"If this entire island was owned by twelve men, your great-grandfather must have owned more than just the land Maggie owns now."

"He did. In fact, at one point he owned most of the land where the village of Harthaven now stands. He divided the land among his sons, and Maggie's father ended up with the land on the peninsula. My grandfather inherited the land bordering the marina, and Great-grandpa's youngest son got the land at the north end of town. I'm surprised you don't remember all of this from history class. It was covered in the fourth grade."

"I guess I wasn't paying attention. My dad moved to the island when he was a young man, so my family wasn't one of the privileged twelve."

I shrugged. "I don't suppose it matters all that much now. The land has mostly been divided into small residential and commercial lots. Still, if Mrs.

Trexler was researching property in the area and she's dead now, it might warrant looking in to."

Chapter 6

Cody and I decided to look more closely at the information Orson had sent to Mrs. Trexler. Although I felt horrible about doing so, I brought Tara her smoothie as promised but then explained that I had to leave again in order to help Cody follow up on Orson's e-mail. The fact that she didn't even look surprised made me feel even worse. Clearly I was a partner who couldn't be counted on. As soon as I helped solve this mystery, I vowed to start being the best business partner ever.

We decided to work at my cabin because I had a computer and Internet set up. Cody stopped by to pick up Rambler before meeting me there. Once he arrived, Cody worked on the information Orson had forwarded while I tried to open the journal, which I hadn't gotten to the day before. The emergency island council meeting was planned for later that evening, and if there was something to find Cody and I wanted to have it before then.

I let Max out for a few minutes, then settled onto the sofa in the living area while Cody sat nearby at the desk where the computer was located. Alice curled up next to me and began to purr while I worked on opening the lock without ruining it. Max seemed content to play with Rambler on the front deck.

"Did you find something?" I asked Cody, who was frowning at the computer screen.

"I'm not sure. Two of the links Orson sent lead to maps of the island." Cody displayed the maps side by side. "One of the maps appears to be at least fifty years old. Maybe older, because it's hand drawn. The other one is recent. It includes the town of Pelican Bay, which isn't on the older map."

I got up from my place on the sofa and walked over to the desk. I looked over Cody's shoulder at the screen he was focused on. The newer map looked like a current one of the island, whereas the other one was old indeed. It showed the division of property that went back to the original settlers.

"Look there." I pointed to the screen. "This shows the settlement of Harthaven, as well as the property lines of the peninsula."

Cody looked back and forth between the two maps. "Mrs. Trexler must have had a reason to want copies of these maps. The old one shows the name of other landowners of the time, but I don't see a Trexler."

"Trexler would have been her married name," I pointed out.

"True. Do we know her maiden name?"

I frowned. "I'm afraid she has always been Mrs. Trexler to me. I'm sure Maggie must know. Or my mom. Hang on and I'll call over to the Bait and Stitch to ask Maggie. If I call my mom I'll never get off the phone."

Cody continued to follow the links while I talked to Maggie, who was at home, not at the shop. It turned out that Haley was interested in learning to sew, and since the Bait and Stitch hadn't been busy, Maggie had brought her home to work on the quilt for the float while Marley held down the fort.

"She's coming over," I informed Cody. "I told her that wasn't necessary, but she's only a hundred yards away and I've piqued her interest. Should we tell her what's going on? I feel like she has the right to know."

Cody shrugged. "She's your aunt, so I guess it's your call."

When Maggie arrived I filled her in on the series of events leading to our being gathered in my cabin staring at maps on a computer screen. I expected her to be furious that Mrs. Trexler had been the one to poison her, or at least had known who had done it, but all the news made her was sad.

"Poor Susan. She must have gotten herself into a tough spot to have agreed to do such a thing."

The fact that the woman had ended up dead seemed to support that supposition.

"I know she lived on the island her whole life. She mentioned it more than once. Do you know if her family goes as far back as the founders?"

"Her great-grandfather was one of the original settlers."

"Do you know his name?" I asked.

"Jedidiah Boyle."

I looked at the old map. There was a plot of land that was labeled as belonging to Boyle. I frowned. "The land that belonged to Mrs. Trexler's family is part of the land Bill Powell bought to build his development. You don't think Mrs. Trexler sold?"

"Her father sold that land a long time ago. It had to have been the new owners who sold."

"Do you know who bought the land from the Boyles?" I asked.

"No, I'm afraid I don't. I do know that the land was subdivided into smaller lots. I suppose if you're really interested you can search the county records."

I looked at the map again. Powell was planning to build his development on land made up of five plots of varying sizes, including two large sections that appeared to have belonged to two of the founding families. Based on the property lines of the old map, the northern section of Bill's proposed development was a large piece of land owned by Jedidiah Boyle at the time the map was drawn, the southern section by a man named Barney Fitzgerald.

"Fitzgerald? That sounds familiar," I commented.

"The Fitzgeralds have all died off or left the island, except for Nora Fitzgerald," Maggie informed me.

I frowned. "I don't think I know her."

"Of course you do. She goes by Nora Bradley now."

"Mayor Bradley's wife owns part of the land Bill Powell plans to develop?" I spat.

"I thought you knew that," Maggie said. "I'm afraid the sales contingency is one of the reasons he's been pushing so hard to have the project approved."

"Sales contingency?" Where had I been that I knew nothing about any of this?

"Bill Powell made each of the landowners an offer that included paying them seventy-five percent of the fair market value of the land up front. If the project is approved he's going to double that amount, which means that each landowner would receive one hundred and fifty percent of the land's fair market value. If the project isn't approved Bill plans to sell the land, and the original owners will be out twenty-five percent of what it was initially valued at. As far as I can see, Bill comes out okay either way. It's the original landowners who stand to lose out if the project isn't approved."

"Have you known this all along?" I asked.

"Of course, dear. I make it my responsibility to know what's going on. I wouldn't be a very good council member if I didn't."

I took a deep breath and tried to gather my thoughts. While I'd been interested in the development, I hadn't been passionate about it one way or the other before Maggie got sick. And then, after she did become ill, I was so busy trying to hold everything together that I hadn't paid a whole lot of attention to the situation. When I found out about the arsenic and began to suspect that the tampering with the tea was related to the project I began to look into it further. I hadn't wanted to bother Maggie with the details because she had been so ill, and it never occurred to me that she knew so much about what was going on.

"Okay, let me be sure I have this straight. Mayor Bradley's wife and whoever bought Mrs. Trexler's family's land have sold to Bill Powell for a lot less than what it's worth up front in the hope of a huge payout in the end?"

"Yes, that's what I just said."

"If the project is blocked these landowners stand to lose a lot of money."

"That's what you just said, only in a different way. Are you closing in on a point?" Maggie asked.

Cody snickered at Maggie's reply. I shot him *the look* before I continued.

"Don't you see? Mayor Bradly has to be behind everything that's going on."

Maggie chuckled. "Why would Sue Trexler be working with Bradley?"

I bit my lip. Maggie had a point. Mrs. Trexler had been very outspoken about not wanting to see the project approved.

"If Mrs. Trexler either tampered with your tea or protected the identity of the person who did, can you think of a reason for her to have done so?" I asked.

Maggie thought about it. "Not really. I certainly didn't have a beef with the woman. I believe she was supporting Francine in the election and I was ahead of Francine in the polls before I got sick, but that's no reason to poison me."

"Her involvement with your illness must have something to do with the development even though the link isn't evident right now. We know she was researching land ownership, she confessed to Father Kilian that she was involved in some way with the tea tampering, and now she's dead. Can we find out who owns the rest of the land Bill purchased?" I asked Cody.

"I'm sure we can," he said. He typed some commands into the computer's browser and pulled up a map of the slice of acreage Bill Powell had acquired. "Bill purchased twenty-two acres in all. Ten of those were owned by Nora Bradley and ten were owned by Tim Davenport. There's also a two-acre parcel owned by Tran Flanders. It appears the land owned by Tim and Tran was once part of what was owned by Mrs. Trexler's grandfather. He originally owned thirty acres, but he divided them into smaller parcels that he sold separately.

Tim Davenport still lived on the island. He was a Realtor and developer who dealt in high-end properties.

"Who is Tran Flanders?" I asked.

Maggie shrugged. "I've never heard of him."

"Can we get more information on him?" I asked Cody.

"We can certainly try."

I looked at the map while Cody continued to search. "If you compare the old map and the new one, it looks like the two acres Tran Flanders owned was once part of a ten-acre parcel owned by Jimmy Lee. Jimmy must have purchased the land from Mrs. Trexler's grandfather and then further divided it."

"I guess that makes sense," Cody acknowledged.

I bit my lip as I compared the maps. "It looks like the owners of the other part of Jimmy Lee's land is Banjo and Summer."

Cody frowned. "Really?"

"Yeah, look." I pointed to the map. "The plot of land just to the west of Bill's development is where Banjo and Summer live."

"You're right," Cody agreed.

"If they bought part of Jimmy Lee's land maybe they know who Tran Flanders is," I suggested

"It couldn't hurt to ask."

"I really need to get back," Maggie announced. "I need to finish up with Halcy and then take her home. She's working out to be such a good helper."

"It's still early," I pointed out. "I don't think her aunt cares how late she's out."

"I know, dear, but I wanted to get to the island council meeting early to let everyone know I'm feeling better and am very much back in the running for one of the open seats. I also want to see if I can't prevent the current council members from killing one another as we work through this mess."

"Cody and I will meet you over there. Would you like me to see to the cats?"

"No, Haley and I will do it before I take her home. She's really very good with them. Even Moose seems to like her, and Moose doesn't like anyone."

"I noticed that. She seems to be some sort of cat whisperer."

After Maggie returned to the house Cody called Banjo, who confirmed that he and Summer owned the lot just to the west of the development. He informed Cody that Jimmy had been an old surfing buddy who'd left him the land when he died. Banjo said he'd actually inherited the land almost ten years ago but never visited the property until he and Summer decided to move to the island eighteen months ago. He'd never met Tran Flanders, nor did he have any idea why Jimmy would have sold off two of the ten acres he owned to this man.

As frustrating as it was, it seemed that instead of finding answers all we'd managed to do was dig up more questions.

By the time Cody and I headed over to the council meeting we'd come to the conclusion that Tran Flanders didn't exist. We'd tried every search engine we could think of, but so far it was no go. Cody was going to try to call Orson again the next day and I was going to break open the lock on the journal if I couldn't manage to pick it by the next morning. We agreed to meet back at my place to compare notes over a late breakfast after I'd picked up Haley for the day, which meant I was going to have to bail on Tara again. Boy, was I going to owe her, *big*. I couldn't think of a single thing she'd want that she didn't already have except for Danny, who had conveniently shown up at the meeting too.

I walked up behind my big brother and put an arm around his shoulder. "Dinner, my place tomorrow night, seven o'clock. Bring the beer." Cody and I had choir practice, but it would be over by then.

Danny hesitated.

"Yes, Tara will be there, and yes, you still have to come," I answered in anticipation of his response. "The two of you have been friends your entire lives. You can't let any weird energy that may have been created by some totally random moment affect that."

Danny still didn't say anything.

"This is not negotiable," I insisted.

Danny started to speak. I could see by the look on his face that he was going to argue.

"I'm invoking the sibling pact."

Danny sighed. "Okay. I'll be there."

I kissed his cheek and retuned to Cody's side.

"Wow," Cody said. "What exactly is the sibling pact?"

"Let's just say that as siblings close in age, you're privy to facts about the other that they might not want known to the general populace. Danny and I agreed a long time ago to keep each other's confidences. The favor thing was added to the pact when we were in high school and there was a situation when he wanted me to do something for him and I refused. He reminded me that he knew all my deepest, darkest secrets and would hate to see them leaked. I agreed to do what he asked of me, but in return he agreed to do what I asked, when I asked it. It's been a lot of years, but I've finally got around to cashing in. Now all I need to do is convince Tara to come, which may mean cashing in some best friend points. You'll be there, won't you?"

"Do you want me to come?" Cody asked.

"Of course. You'll act as a buffer. Besides, you can help me with the cooking. I thought we'd head over right after choir practice."

"Mr. Parsons is coming home," Cody reminded me.

"I'll see if Banjo and Summer will sit with him. He mentioned on the phone that they missed hanging out and watching soaps with him."

Banjo and Summer live down the beach from Mr. Parsons. They don't have a television, so they go over to watch his.

"Okay, if Banjo and Summer can sit with Mr. Parsons I'm in," Cody said.

"It looks like the meeting is about to start," I commented. "This should be interesting."

Chapter 7

Wednesday, June 3

I got up at first light the next morning so I could take Max for a run before I picked up Haley. It was foggy this morning, so the view we'd been enjoying the past couple of weeks of sunshine was limited to a few feet in any direction. The forecast was for rain, so I wasn't holding out much hope of cooking dinner out on the deck as I'd originally planned.

My cell phone rang just as Max and I were returning from our run. It was Doris Rutherford, who was not only the queen bee of the Madrona Island gossip line but a frequent visitor to the quilting circle that seemed to find a reason to convene almost every day at the Bait and Stitch.

"I'm so sorry to bother you early in the morning," she began, "but I noticed that the feral cat that's been hanging around has had kittens. I believe they're in the crawl space under my house. I can hear meowing when I'm in the kitchen. It's such a cold and damp day; I thought maybe you'd want to trap them and take them back to the sanctuary."

I looked at my watch. If I hurried I'd have time to rescue the cat and kittens before I was due to pick up Haley. "I'll be right over."

I headed over to the cat sanctuary to gather the supplies I would need. It was a dark morning and thick black clouds had descended on the island from the west. I was willing to bet we were in for a heck of a storm.

Doris lived on a street that was just inland from the water. The lot in front of her was vacant, so she had an excellent view, but it looked as if that lot was part of the property Bill Powell planned to use for his project.

"Thank you for coming so quickly," Doris greeted me at her front door. "I can hear the cats below my floor, so I'm hoping the mom is with the kittens. They can't be more than a week old, so they really need to be kept together."

"Do you know how the cat got under the house?" I asked.

"There's a vent on the side of the house that has a missing screen. I imagine she got in through there."

"Let's block the vent before I head under. It'll be easier to catch her if she can't get out from under the house."

"I think there's some old lumber on the side of the house. We can use that."

Doris followed me as I walked around the house. "I've always enjoyed this view," I commented. "Didn't there used to be a house on that lot?"

"There was. Bill tore it down after he purchased the property. The land belonged to Tim Davenport, although he didn't live on it."

I knew Tim owned a large home on the other side of the island.

"Watch the opening at the front of the house while I crawl under to see if I can get both Mama and babies. We don't want Mom getting away," I said.

"Will do."

I really hated crawling around in the small space, which barely provided enough room to scoot through on my stomach. I had to control my imagination, which was producing the feeling of creepy crawly things having a party in my thick hair. Luckily, I was able to rescue Mom and kittens without too much trouble. There were four in all: two black, an orange, and a gray and white mix.

I chatted with Doris for a few more minutes and then headed over to pick up Haley.

"They're so tiny," Haley said after we got them settled in at the sanctuary. She gently helped to transfer the kittens into the nursery box I had prepared.

"Yeah, they can't be more than a few days old. It's a good thing Mrs. Rutherford heard them. It can get pretty cold at night even in June."

"I wish I could have a kitten." Haley sighed. "If I could, I would want one that looked just like that orange one."

"You don't have any animals?"

"No. I can't with Mama being so sick and all."

I squeezed the girl's hand in a show of comfort.

"How did things work out with Maggie yesterday?"

The girl lit up like a Christmas tree. "It was so fun. She's no nice, and so is Marley. They're teaching me to sew, and they're even letting me help with the float. Maggie said she would teach me to fish, but I think I'll stick with sewing for now."

I laughed. "Maggie loves to fish, but I have to admit it isn't a passion I share. Of course, I'm not much good with a needle and thread either."

"Maggie told me that. She told me that she didn't have any kids and none of her nieces liked to sew, so she was going to have so much fun teaching me."

I hugged the girl. "I think you, Miss Haley, are going to be very good for Maggie's recovery."

"She told me she'd been sick. I hope she's not sick like Mama."

"Maggie's getting better and will be back to her old self in no time. How about we take care of the cats and then I'll walk you up to the house? I'm sure Maggie is looking forward to spending the day with you."

Haley and I cleaned the sanctuary and fed the cats and then I turned her over to Maggie and returned to my cabin, where I quickly put the egg pie I'd assembled the previous evening in the oven before approaching the task of building a fire in the fireplace. It was a damp as well as a cool morning, and a fire would take the chill out of the lightly insolated cabin.

After I built the fire I poured myself a cup of coffee and sat down on the sofa to drink it. I'd finally managed to get the journal open at two minutes to midnight, only to find that it was completely empty except for two pages. On one page were written four sets of six numbers each. On the other was a string of letters that didn't appear to be related in any way. I had no clue what either might mean. I supposed they could be codes of some sort. Mrs. Trexler hadn't seemed the cloak and dagger sort, but she also didn't seem the sort to get mixed up in a conspiracy that left one person sick and herself dead. I screwed up my face as I tried to make sense of what I was looking at.

"The numbers are coordinates," Cody said from behind me.

I almost jumped out of my skin when he spoke. "I didn't hear you come in. How long have you been standing there?"

"Not long. I learned to walk quietly when I was in the Navy."

"Coordinates for what?" I asked.

Cody looked at the numbers again. "I can tell they're from around here, but I don't know where exactly. We could easily find out if you want to take a field trip."

"I'm game." I looked out the window. It had started to drizzle, and visibility was still as bad as it had been that morning. "Although I suppose it can wait until after we eat. The egg pie I made should be done by now. Help yourself to some coffee."

Cody headed into the kitchen.

"Any idea what the letters mean?' I asked.

"Not without looking at them longer. I'm guessing it's some sort of code."

"That's what I was thinking. I have no idea how we're ever going to figure it out without some kind of a key."

"Maybe she left one," Cody suggested.

"Maybe. Did you get hold of Orson?" I asked.

"I left him a message, but he hasn't called me back."

"I was hoping the journal would tell me who Mrs. Trexler was working with. I really believe that figuring that out could be the answer to figuring everything out."

I looked out the window as the wind shifted, sending the rain into the windows at the front of the cabin. "It looks like it's getting worse. I'm not sure we'll be able to take our field trip today."

"A little rain never hurt anyone," Cody teased.

He made some toast as I sliced the pie. We both refilled our coffee cups and then sat down at the kitchen table, which was placed against one of the windows that was being pelted with rain. Max crawled under my chair as thunder rumbled from a distance.

"I hope Danny isn't out on the water this morning," Cody said as the waves crashed onto the beach.

"He usually doesn't leave on his first charter until noon and he's really good about checking the weather beforehand. I imagine he'll need to reschedule unless the storm blows through quickly. So what are you plans for today?"

"I'm supposed to pick up Mr. Parsons from the hospital later this morning, and then I was going to work on my business plan for the newspaper. I'd like to make a decision about it in the next day or two. Other than joining you for the very awkward dinner party you invited me to, I have no other plans."

Alice jumped up onto the table and lay down.

"Tables are for eating, not for sleeping," I said to the cat, who ignored me.

Cody laughed as Alice rolled over onto her back. "It seems like she's calling the shots around here."

"She does seem to have strong opinions about what we should be doing. I'm surprised she isn't knocking things off the counter or pulling books off shelves."

"She being a nuisance?"

"Not really. It's just her way of communicating. She's the one who brought my attention to the journal in the first place. She seems to have a way of bringing me what I need just when I need it."

Cody reached over and removed something from her long fur. "Like sticky notes stuck to stomach fur?"

I took the small note from Cody. It had a single word on it, written in Mrs. Trexler's handwriting. "It must have fallen out of the journal." I looked at Alice and smiled as she jumped off the table and went to lie in front of the fire.

"It could be the key," Cody speculated.

I looked at the note and frowned. It said FS6-P7. "Okay, so what could it mean?" I asked.

"I'm not sure. Let's finish eating and then see if we can't figure it out."

We were no closer to figuring out the code than we'd been when we started by the time Cody had to leave to pick up Mr. Parsons. I did the dishes and then tossed my raincoat over my head so as not to get completely soaked as I ran across the lawn to Maggie's. Normally, she would be in town at this time of day, but I could see that her lights were on, so I'd decided to check in on her.

Like all three of the homes on the peninsula, Maggie's was massive, three stories with so many bedrooms it was hard to keep track. I found it odd that while each of the three houses had been built by men with multitudes of children and grandchildren in mind, each currently housed a single resident. Maggie had never married, nor had Mr. Parsons. Francine Rivers had married as a young woman but had become a childless young widow before her first anniversary. Between the three houses there had to be thirty bedrooms, yet most were empty now.

Of course, I lived in Maggie's guesthouse, and Cody had moved into Mr. Parsons's mausoleum of a house. As far as I knew, Mr. Parsons didn't have any family he was close to, so I wondered what would become of the house once he passed on. When Siobhan was engaged to Finn Maggie had made a comment about leaving the young couple her house so they could fill up all those empty rooms with children, but now that my big sister lived in Seattle I wasn't sure what her plans for the property were.

"Close the door before the rain blows in," Maggie instructed as I struggled against the strong wind.

"It's really coming down out there," I commented as I hung my raincoat on a peg near the front door.

"They're calling for wind and strong rain throughout the day. Marley and I decided not to open. Haley is upstairs working on her sewing project, and I want to get started on my speech. Besides, I doubt anyone is out looking for fishing supplies in this weather."

"How's your speech coming along?" I asked.

At the meeting the night before, the island council had voted to delay the election for a month so that everyone who wanted to run had a chance to submit their paperwork. All those who decided to run for the open seats were going to be given the opportunity to tell the island residents why they felt they would be the best suited to fill the positions at the next meeting, which was scheduled in two weeks. The plan was a compromise neither side was entirely happy about it, but it seemed to me to be the best option.

"It's pretty good, if I don't say so myself."

"I'm sure you'll have no problem winning one of the seats now that you're back to your old self," I said as I stepped in front of the fire in order to take the chill off.

"I hope you're right. Now that there are two open seats there's a lot of chatter about additional candidates. By the time all's been said and done, I wouldn't be surprised if there aren't three or four additional islanders throwing their hats into the ring alongside the four original candidates. It could splinter the vote to the point where a dark horse could win."

"You think so?"

Maggie shrugged. "I've seen it happen."

"Are you worried?"

"Nah. No use wasting energy on things I can't control. I'd much rather enjoy my time with Haley."

"It's really nice that you've taken such an interest in her. She's a great kid, and I think she really needs to have a project to keep her mind off things."

"I'm having the best time with her," Maggie admitted. "For the first time in my life I find that I'm wondering if I didn't miss out on having children of my own."

"Thanks a lot," I joked.

Maggie laughed. "You know I adore you and your sisters, but Haley seems to be interested in many of the same things I am, whereas the three of you never showed any interest in sewing or fishing at all."

"Haley loves the sewing, but I'm not sure she's all that keen on fishing. She'll probably be too polite to tell you, but I thought you should know."

"I'll keep it in mind."

"If you need to work on your speech I can take Haley today," I offered.

"The girl doesn't seem to need a lot of supervision. She's been sewing away since she's been here and has barely made a peep. If I had to guess I'd say that having an ill mother has taught her how to be invisible."

"Yeah, it sounds like she's had a tough time. Her whole family has. I think she knows how to be self-sufficient. By the way, as long as I'm here, I wanted to ask if FS6-P7 means anything to you."

Maggie thought about it. "I believe FS is the old designation for parcel numbers. They've since been modified, but unless I'm mistaken, FS once stood for Family Share. Why do you ask?"

I explained what I'd found in the journal.

Maggie looked at the numbers and letters I had copied down and stuck in my pocket.

"I don't know what the letters mean, but if these are coordinates at least one of them falls within the project boundaries for the condo development."

"Are you sure?"

"Absolutely."

"How do you know that?"

"I told you, I've done my homework. I'd have to look at a map, but I'd say that the two numbers at the top of the page represent coordinates that fall within the boundaries of the northern end of the project."

"And the other two?"

"I'd say they fall to the west of it."

I knew this was going to be important, but at this point I wasn't at all sure what it might mean.

Chapter 8

Cody and I decided to cancel choir practice for that day once it became evident that the storm wasn't going to let up any time soon. I called Sister Mary to inform her of our decision, and she agreed it was best not to ask people to go out in the storm. Tara arrived at the cabin with Bandit zipped into her jacket at about the same time Cody showed up alone. I thought he might bring Rambler, but now that Mr. Parsons was home he'd left the dog to comfort the old man.

Danny lives on his boat, so he'd planned to spend the night in one of Maggie's guest rooms, as he often did when it stormed. He was up at the house dropping off his overnight bag before heading over to the cabin for the meal we'd planned.

"Storm seems to be getting worse," Cody commented as he took off his wet jacket.

"Yeah, it's a bad one. Did Banjo and Summer get to Mr. Parsons's okay?"

"Yeah. They're going to stay over so they don't have to drive all the way home in the rain."

"That's a good idea."

Although Banjo and Summer lived just down the beach from Mr. Parsons, it was quite a long way by road. The three properties on the peninsula were serviced by a road that connected to the main highway. While Banjo and Summer could walk down the beach to Mr. Parsons's house in less than fifteen minutes, to drive between the two properties you had to go all the way back to Pelican Bay, drive through town, and then catch the coast road along the stretch of beach that Bill Powell hoped to develop. If the development was approved Banjo and Summer would have to drive through the development in order to access their property.

I'd decided not to bring up the murder investigation until after we ate, and to avoid the topic of the unfortunate kiss altogether. As soon as each guest arrived I put them to work in order to avoid even a moment of uncomfortable silence. Tara and I put out the food for the burrito bar I'd planned, while Danny made the margaritas and Cody set out the chips and salsa. During the meal, which consisted of both beef and chicken as well as three kinds of cheese, both hot and mild salsa, and my special homemade guacamole, the conversation remained light and casual. By the time the third pitcher of margaritas was being passed around any discomfort that might have existed had been replaced with the comfortable camaraderie of four longtime friends sharing a meal.

"This storm reminds me of that time we unwisely decided to take Aiden's boat for a joy ride when we were in high school," Danny commented as a sheet of rain slammed into the window at the front of the cabin.

"Looking back, it's a miracle we weren't all killed," Tara commented. "I can't ever remember being more terrified in my entire life."

Danny, Cody, Tara, me, and six other friends had all borrowed Aiden's boat without his permission, which had been a dumb thing to do in the first place. When we'd set out for the day it had been sunny with a light breeze, but before we knew what hit us, a storm had blown in, causing the gentle sea to turn into a raging pool of crashing waves and powerful surges. Somehow Danny had managed to sail the boat to an island that had once been inhabited but had since become deserted. We'd stayed on the island for two days while we waited out the storm. Tara might remember the event as terrifying, but I had many fond memories of our short stay on that island.

"Do you remember how run-down that old cabin was that we finally decided to camp out in?" I asked.

"It was more than run-down." Cody laughed. "It didn't even have a complete roof. It's a miracle the whole thing didn't blow over on us."

"It was cold," Tara said.

"And wet," Danny added.

"And awesome," I joined in.

"Awesome?" Danny responded. "Are you thinking of the same trip we are?"

"I am, and, yes, it was cold and wet and terrifying, but I also remember building a fire in the old stone fireplace and telling ghost stories all night. We didn't have enough blankets to go around, so we all had to share, and the food each of us had with us didn't really make a meal, but we had fun making up interesting taste combinations. I suppose there was a level of discomfort, but I remember it as being fun."

"It was fun," Cody seconded.

"In a Stephen King horror story kind of way," Tara countered. "Let's not forget about the fact that Cody told everyone that the reason the island was deserted was because an escaped mental patient got lost in a storm, landed on the island, and killed every man, woman, and child living there."

Cody laughed again. "I'd heard that chicks were more apt to put out when they were scared, so I made up the story—which really worked out, judging by all the creaking and groaning created by the wind and rain."

"You are such a pig." I tossed a napkin at Cody's head.

"Maybe, but I got to second base with Cheryl Fremeyer."

I tried to scowl but couldn't help but grin at the memory of that long-ago night. I'm sure I was terrified at the time, but every time the wind howls and the house creaks I remember Cody telling his tale by the light of the dancing fire.

"Does anyone know why the island really was deserted?" I asked.

"It was wiped out in a storm," Danny informed us. "I guess the residents decided not to rebuild. I don't think there were many people living there in the first place."

"It was sort of spooky, with all those empty buildings," I said.

A huge wave crashing onto the shore thundered, making us all jump.

"That was a big one," Tara commented. "Do you think your cabin is set back far enough?"

"It's been here for years and has weathered worse storms, so I imagine we're okay. I have brownie sundaes for dessert. Anyone interested?"

Everyone was.

We finished our meal and Tara and I did the dishes while Danny and Cody let Max out for a quick run. After Max returned we all settled onto the sofa in front of the fire. Cody and I quickly got Danny and

Tara up to speed before asking for their help with the encrypted message in the journal.

"Let me see that." Tara took the journal from my hand. She bit her lip as she studied it. The message read: DERREFSNARTDEYEVRUSDLOS

"Do you have a piece of paper and a pencil?" she asked.

"Uh, sure. Somewhere."

"Never mind." Tara dug into her shoulder bag and pulled out the pad she'd been using for making notes on the remodel. She wrote the letters both forward and backward and then added three dashes.

"It says sold, surveyed, and transferred."

She showed me the piece of paper she'd used to work out the puzzle. Sure enough, it said: SOLD/SURVEYED/TRANSFERRED

"How did you figure that out so quickly?" I asked.

Tara shrugged. "I have a logical mind that sees patterns in random sources of data. Both Maggie and Cody were certain the number sets were coordinates, so my guess is that Mrs. Trexler came across some information someone didn't want found."

"Like Bill Powell," I guessed.

"Like Bill Powell," Tara agreed.

"The piece that doesn't fit is that there's no way Mrs. Trexler was working with Bill Powell," Danny reminded us.

I nodded.

"There are people other than Bill who will benefit from the project," Cody reminded us. "Just as there are people who'll be harmed. When we looked at the map today it seemed clear there were several landowners who stand to make a bundle by selling their land if the project goes through. There are also a handful of landowners whose ocean view will be eliminated by the condominiums if they're built."

"Cody has a point," I agreed. "I went by Doris Rutherford's today to rescue a feral cat and her kittens. Doris lives on a street just behind the land Bill plans to build on. At the moment she has an excellent view, but if Bill builds his condos she'll just be looking at walls."

"Who else lives on that street?" Tara asked.

Danny laid out the maps Cody had printed from the links Orson had provided to Mrs. Trexler. Tara stood next to him as they studied the property lines. "It looks like there are five landowners whose property butts up to the parcels Bill Powell is planning to build on," Danny informed us.

"Doris Rutherford lives there." I pointed to a large plot of land.

"And Pete Baxter lives next to her," Danny added.

"Pete was talking to Mrs. Trexler on the day she was killed," I informed the others. "He said he was at the ferry to pick up the mail and just ran into her, but he did seem sort of fidgety when he was telling me what had occurred."

"Who owns the other parcels?" Cody asked.

"Banjo and Summer own the one that lines the coast," I said. "The way their property is situated, they'll lose part of their ocean view but not all of it. Still, their property values are going to drop quite a bit once those condos are built."

"Neither Banjo nor Summer seems the type to care all that much about property values," Cody said.

"That's true," I acknowledged.

"Banjo once mentioned to me that Byron Maxwell lived on the property to his south, so that must be his lot there." Danny pointed to a spot on the map. Byron was a member of the island council who had spoken out against the project. Originally, there had been three council members against and two for the project. Mayor Bradley was a strong supporter and stood to make a lot of money from the sale of his property. Keith Weaver, Gary Pixley, and Byron had all voiced their opposition to the condos. Keith was dead. Gary had been bribed into resigning from the council and leaving the island, which left Byron as the sole member of the council who was still against the project.

"So who owns the fifth plot of land?" I asked.

Everyone stared at the map, but none of us knew for certain.

"We could drive over there after the storm lets up and take a look," I suggested.

Everyone jumped as a tree branch hit the side of my small cabin.

"It's really bad out there," Cody said.

I looked out the front window. The normally gentle waves had swelled to ten times their usual height before crashing onto the shore. While the scene outside was terrifying, the one inside my warm little cabin brought contentment to my heart. Tara was sitting on the sofa in front of the fire with Bandit in her lap. Danny was next to her, holding Alice. Cody sat on the floor with Max. There was a spot on the sofa next to Danny waiting for my return. I thought about Maggie alone up in the house and hoped she was okay.

"Maybe we should all head up to the big house," I said. "There are plenty of guest rooms, and I don't want to leave Maggie alone in the storm."

"Marley is with Maggie and Haley is spending the night," Danny informed me. "The three of them are discussing patterns for the float. Francine was over there as well when I dropped my things off. It looked like they were going to settle in for a long evening of girl talk."

"Oh, then maybe we'll just stay here," I decided. "Trying to figure out who killed Mrs. Trexler sounds a lot more interesting than talking about fabrics and patterns."

Chapter 9

Thursday, June 4

The storm had blown through by the next morning, so after my exercise class with Tara I decided to take the ferry to the county seat to look at the official plot maps in the assessor's office. The clues in Mrs. Trexler's journal had said sold/surveyed/transferred. That had to mean something. Something important. If FS6-P7 did refer to a plot of land, as Maggie suspected, surely the people in the county office would be able to give me the history of the property.

"Caitlin Hart," John Goodwin, one of the employees of the Washington State ferry system greeted me. "I wasn't sure it was you standing over there until I saw your van parked at the front of the vessel. Are you heading to an adoption clinic?"

"No, I have to look up some stuff at the county office. How's your daughter doing?"

John's daughter had just had a baby. Her third.

"She's doing better. It was a tough labor and delivery, but both Mama and baby seem to be doing fine. Now that she's feeling better, she's agreed to let my grandson have that orange kitten we talked about the last time we spoke."

"That's wonderful. And the timing is good; she's ready to go to her forever home."

"I can come by your place tomorrow to pick her up," John offered. "Say around noon?"

"Actually, Tara and I received the funding we've been waiting for to do the remodel on the old cannery and I really should be there to help out. I can bring the kitten with me if you want to meet me there."

"Sounds like we have a plan. So now that we've dispensed with the chitchat, are you ready to tell me about your latest mishap?" John's eyes seemed to twinkle as he spoke. I don't know what there is about him, but of all the people I know, he's the one who's most apt to get me to spill my deepest, darkest secrets.

"I'm really not supposed to talk about it," I answered.

"Yup. I can see why there are those who might want to keep another murder quiet for the time being."

"How did you know I found another body?" I asked. As far as I knew, the only people who knew about my discovery were Cody, Danny, Tara, and, of course, Finn.

I waited for John's answer to my inquiry. He shrugged. "Doing what I do, you hear things," he evaded.

"Doing what you do?" I raised a single eyebrow. It wasn't like working on a ferry was the type of job that would lend itself to being privy to sensitive information.

"Bella and Tansy came over on an earlier ferry," he explained. "They might have mentioned a few facts about your latest mystery."

"But how did they . . . never mind." I should know by now that Bella and Tansy would be aware of what was going on. They seemed to know everything. I'm not sure how they do what they do, but they're two of the most awesome women I know, so I just accept it without asking.

"I'm sure Bella and Tansy already told you whatever it was they felt you needed to know," I said. "If you don't mind I'd really like to keep my promise to Finn, at least for the time being."

"As you should."

I pulled my hair back into a knot as the crosswind shifted and blew strands across my face.

"I ran into Camden Bradford yesterday." John changed the subject. "He was taking the ferry from Seattle to Bremerton."

"How did he seem?" I asked. I'd thought of him often since his brother-in-law had been arrested and he'd quit his temporary job.

"Things have been tough for him, but he seemed to be dealing with them well. It seems he's planning to take his sister on a trip. He indicated she was taking the situation really hard. Feel bad for the guy and his family."

"Yeah," I sighed, "Me too. I've thought about it a lot, and I can understand how people can be propelled into doing things they wouldn't ordinarily do when large amounts of money are involved."

"Money is a strong motivator," John agreed, "By the way, I've been meaning to ask you how Maggie is doing."

"Better now that she knows what was making her sick. She's not quite back to her old self, but she seems to be improving a little bit every day. We expect a full recovery."

"Did you ever find out who was tampering with her tea?" John asked.

I hesitated.

"I see you know but can't say," John commented.

"Yeah, something like that. I've been meaning to ask you about Pete Baxter." I realized a minute too late that my abrupt segue probably gave John a clue to who was behind the tea tampering. I have a tendency to speak before I think, but even if John put two and two together he can keep a secret when one needs to be kept.

"What about Pete Baxter?" John asked.

"Does he pick up the mail every morning?"

"Like clockwork."

"And Susan Trexler—have you seen her picking up packages as well?"

John frowned. "No, I can't say that I have. Why do you ask?"

"Everett Conroy told me he saw Mrs. Trexler with Mr. Baxter on Friday morning. I asked Mr. Baxter about it and he said he was picking up the mail and ran into her, and that she didn't take the ferry but just came on board to pick up a box and then left the terminal with someone in a blue sedan."

John tapped his chin as he thought about the situation. "I don't remember seeing her, but I suppose I might have been busy loading the cars that were boarding. I guess she might have met someone who was already on the ferry who handed it off to her. I know I wasn't holding a package for her."

I watched as a pod of whales swam up alongside the ferry as it turned to approach the terminal.

"Is there any other staff person who might have been holding a package for her?" I asked.

"Not on that particular day. I work the car deck on Fridays, and if there's a package to be transferred it's kept in the office there. I doubt one of the guys from upstairs would have agreed to meet up with her. Having said that, there are a lot of folks like yourself who make the ride on the car deck, so it's plausible that there was someone waiting onboard to meet her. You seem worried."

"Yeah, I have a few things on my mind," I told him as the ferry slowed for its approach.

"I'd like to stay to chat with you about it, but it looks like I'm up," John announced. "Have a nice day on the island, and maybe I'll see you on the return trip."

Like Pelican Bay, the county seat is made up of cute shops and delicious restaurants that serve the community as well as cater to the tourists who come over on the ferry. Normally, I love to walk around the charming little town, but today I was on a mission to find out what it was Susan Trexler was referring to with the code she'd left in her journal.

The clerk at the assessor's office was very helpful in providing the maps and documentation I needed. It appeared I had at my fingertips the means to solve the puzzle, now I just needed to make some sort of sense of what I was looking at.

The maps I was given were much like the ones Cody had found when he followed the links provided by Orson. The modern map showed the island as it now was, which included the town of Pelican Bay, while the older, hand-drawn map showed only the small settlement at Harthaven. The land parcels were numbered but didn't resemble the number we'd found on the sticky note. I frowned as I studied the information in front of me. My gut told me there was something to find; the problem was I had no idea what I was looking for.

"Does FS6-P7 mean anything to you?" I asked the clerk, who had returned to work at the counter while I spread out the maps on a nearby table.

"Sure, if you're asking about the historical distribution of land on Madrona Island."

"Yes, that's what I'm asking about."

"Then you'll need another map. Hold on and I'll get it."

I fidgeted while the clerk went into the back room. I hadn't thought it would be this easy. Of course, I had no idea if this particular clue would lead anywhere, but at least I felt I was making progress.

"This is a map that shows the original family shares." The clerk rolled out an old map on the counter. There were sectioned-off pieces of the island with codes beginning with FS on each of them.

"Can you show me how to read it?" I asked.

"FS stands for family share," the clerk began. "As you know, Madrona Island was originally settled by twelve families. When the founding families got ready to divide up the land they decided to section the island into twenty-acre plots. Each of the founding fathers had the opportunity to choose land one plot at a time, which they felt was a more equitable way to divide things up, because some parts of the island were more valuable than others."

"Which explains why my family owns land on several different parts of the island," I realized.

"Exactly. Each of the founding fathers was assigned a family number. The key is on the bottom of the map."

I looked where the clerk was pointing. My great-grandfather was assigned FS1, and Mrs. Trexler's grandfather was assigned FS6.

"The island was divided and then the men took turns making selections. I assume a good deal of negotiating went on between the men if one person wanted to secure a large tract of land. I've studied this, and it looks as if they sometimes traded away a round in order to obtain a coveted piece of land. If you look closely, you'll see that the end result isn't an equal division of twelve."

"Okay, so FS6-P7 would stand for family share six, plot seven?"

"Exactly. Which is right there." The clerk pointed to a twenty-acre parcel that Mrs. Trexler's father had subdivided into two ten acre parcels he sold to Jimmy Lee and Tim Davenport.

Just above that plot of land was FS4-P6, which had been owned by Grover Cloverdale's great-grandfather, and above that was FS3-P5, which was owned by Nora Bradley's grandfather. The plots were long, with only the very west edge meeting the water. This was the acreage Bill Powell was interested in.

"So Nora Bradley's grandfather was FS3," I confirmed.

"Yes, it appears so."

Based on the original map, the Fitzgerald family had owned prime pieces of land all over the island, but it appeared Nora herself only owned the twenty-acre parcel on which the house she lived in with the mayor was situated: the land they planned to sell, or had sold, to Bill Powell. It appeared that all of the land once owned by Mrs. Trexler's family had been sold off over the years, so all she'd owned was the house she lived in.

"And did Grover Cloverdale sell this plot to Bill Powell?" I asked.

The land I was referring to had been assigned to Grover Cloverdale's grandfather and was between plots assigned to Nora Bradley and Mrs. Trexler's grandfathers.

"I'm not sure. Let me check."

I looked around the utilitarian room while the clerk conducted his search. The walls were painted white and lined with large file cabinets. There was a counter that held a computer and seemed to act as a divider between the reception area, where tables and chairs had been set out for people to use while reviewing the records, and the offices in the back.

"It appears that Grover Cloverdale sold the land to Tim Davenport three years ago," the clerk informed me. "Tim Davenport sold it to Bill Powell two years ago, along with ten acres he'd purchased from Evan Boyle."

Evan Boyle must have been Mrs. Trexler's father; this meant that of the twenty-two acres Bill Powell purchased, Nora Bradley had owned ten, Tim Davenport had owned ten, and Tran Flanders had owned two.

While I found the evolution of land ownership on Madrona Island to be interesting, it was really just the twenty acres that comprised FS6-P7 that I was interested in at this point.

"Would you have an ownership history of each parcel?" I asked.

"I should. Which one are you interested in?"

"This one." I pointed to P7.

"Give me a few minutes and I'll see what I can find."

I continued to study the map. It was fascinating how much ownership of the property on the island had changed over the years. Everyone was up in arms over Bill Powell's condo project, but this certainly wasn't the first time land had been purchased to construct a development on the island. The land mass where the village of Harthaven now stood had once been owned by just two men, one of whom was my great-great-grandfather. Then it had been divided into smaller lots and sold to individual families who wanted to build homes and start businesses. The same thing had happened to the area where Pelican Bay now stood. When the building on the wharf was actually a cannery the area hadn't been considered prime residential property. Then the cannery closed and the ferry arrived and the landowners had turned their acreage into lots they sold for what I assume was a massive amount of money.

As I studied the more current map, I could see there were only a few large plots of land still intact. Prior to this revelation I'd found myself siding with those who wanted to block the project, but maybe new development was simply part of the island's evolution.

I looked up as the clerk returned to the counter. "I found part of what you're looking for, but it appears I'm missing one or more documents."

"What do you mean?" I asked.

The clerk handed me a folder. "Here's where Jedidiah Boyle deeded the twenty acres that were designated P7 to his son." The man then handed me a second folder. "And here's where the son subdivided it and sold half to Jimmy Lee and half to Tim Davenport."

"What's missing?" I asked.

"I found the document where Jimmy left the land to Rupert Reynolds, and here's the one where Bill Powell bought the westernmost two acres from Tran Flanders, but I don't see where Rupert Reynolds sold the two acres to Tran Flanders in the first place."

"Wait; who's Rupert Reynolds?"

"The current owner of this land." The man pointed to the plot he was referring to.

"Banjo's real name is Rupert Reynolds?" I laughed.

"I suppose, if this Banjo is the current owner of the land."

"What do you mean, you can't find where Rupert Reynolds sold the property to Tran Flanders? Banjo is under the assumption that Jimmy sold the property to Tran Flanders before he passed."

The clerk looked at the documents again. "I don't think so. Mr. Lee passed away ten years ago. Mr. Reynolds inherited the property at that time. According to the records, the ten acres were intact. Bill Powell bought the westernmost two acres from Tran Flanders two years ago. I haven't found any paperwork transferring the property, but Mr. Powell had the land surveyed before he purchased it, and the survey report clearly states that the property belongs to Tran Flanders. This tells me that sometime between ten and two years ago Tran Flanders obtained the property. Your Mr. Reynolds must have sold or transferred it to him."

"Can I have copies of all this?" I asked.

"Certainly. Just give me a few minutes."

It seemed the only thing to do was to have a conversation with Banjo. The guy *was* a hippie before all else, and he *did* smoke a lot of weed. Maybe he'd lost the land in a poker game or something and didn't even remember doing so.

Chapter 10

When I got back to the island on the ferry I noticed Tara was still working at Coffee Cat Books. I felt even worse than I already did that I hadn't helped out all week while Tara had been putting in long hours every day. I decided to stop in to drop off the "I'm sorry" tarts I'd purchased from her favorite bakery, which was just down the street from the assessor's office.

"I brought you tarts," I said with a smile.

"What kind?" Tara took the bag and peeked inside.

"A variety. How's the remodel going?"

"So well that I'm afraid to say that we could be ready to open in half the time I'd forecast for fear of jinxing the speed with which this is all coming together."

"Everything looks really nice. I should be able to help you tomorrow."

"How's the investigation coming along?" Tara asked.

I looked around the room. There were still several contractors working on replacing the windows. "Maybe we can talk about it later. Do you want to come by for dinner?"

"Actually," Tara beamed, "I have a date."

"A date? Not with Danny?"

"No, not with Danny. Danny and I had a long chat, and we both decided that our friendship is too valuable to mess with, so we're going to forget the kiss ever happened and continue on with our lives. I decided that what I really needed was to refocus my romantic energy, so when the electrician asked me if I wanted to have dinner I told him that I'd love to." Tara looked at her watch. "I really should be getting home to change. I don't suppose you can stick around and lock up when the guys are done with the windows?"

"I'd be happy to." I really wanted to head straight over to Mr. Parsons's and talk to Banjo, but I did owe Tara, so closing up was the least I could do. "Do I know this electrician?"

"I doubt it. His name is Carl Prescott and he's new to the island. He bought Shoreline Electric from Albert when he retired."

"And you like him?"

Tara shrugged. "I'm not saying I'd want to marry the guy, but he is nice and good-looking, and I could use a distraction. I guess you heard Danny has asked Melanie to the Founders Day dance."

"Actually, I hadn't heard. I know he likes her, but to be honest, I'm not sure what he sees in her."

"I'm sure it has something to do with her cup size." Tara sighed. "But who Danny dates or does not date is not my business."

"I'm glad you feel that way. Trying to understand Danny's dating choices could make you nuts."

"Tell me about it."

I hugged Tara. "I'm glad you met a nice guy. Have a wonderful time tonight. And don't worry about a thing. I'll take care of everything."

"Just lock up when the guys are done," Tara instructed. "There's no need to do anything else."

"Afraid I might make a decision without you?" I teased.

"Exactly."

"Don't worry; I'm just going to sit on the bench out front while I call Cody. I promise not to make any decisions without you."

Tara hugged me. "Okay, thanks. I'll see you tomorrow."

My conversation with Cody revealed that he had Max with him at Mr. Parsons's house, but Banjo and Summer had already left for the day. They'd watched their soap and then decided to head into town to open Ship Wreck for a few hours. I checked with the guys installing the windows, who reported that they had another hour of work at least. I told them I had a quick errand to run and would be back in plenty of time to lock up. I jogged down the street to the colorful shop with the red door and entered to find Banjo in a heated conversation with Doris Rutherford.

"We'll talk later," Doris said to Banjo. I wasn't sure if that was a promise or a threat. Banjo simply shrugged as the woman gathered her bags and left the property without even acknowledging my presence.

"What's her deal?" I asked.

"She has her panties in a knot because she thinks I sold out to Bill Powell. The woman is a nutcase. I'd never sell to that land grabber. Summer and I enjoy our solitude and we're no happier than Doris is about the development, but for some reason she isn't seeing it."

"I imagine she's referring to the property that at some point was sold or transferred to Tran Flanders." It occurred to me that if Doris knew about Tran Flanders, she must be looking into the ownership of the land Bill Powell was planning to build on as well. I wondered if that was a significant fact. She'd obviously done enough digging to know that Banjo had at one time owned the land. Of course she did stand to suffer a huge drop in the value of her property if the project went through, so her interest would make sense.

"Who's Tran Flanders?" Banjo asked.

"Remember we asked you the other day if you knew someone by that name?"

Banjo thought about it. "Yeah, I remember you asking me something like that, but I'm pretty sure I never met the guy, and I certainly didn't sell him any property."

I leaned against the counter as I worked out my approach to the situation. Banjo was an intelligent man, but his attention span was even shorter than mine, and most times you had to sort of steer him through a conversation.

"Would you mind telling me about Jimmy Lee and how it is that you came to own the property that was once his?"

"Summer and I met Jimmy maybe fifteen years ago in Baja. He was a free spirit who liked to follow the waves, the same as us, so we started traveling together. I guess he was some sort of businessman who had a lot of money before he decided that life was too short to waste it on meetings and endless obligations. At some point during our travels I mentioned to him that Summer and I wanted to live on the beach when we finally decided to settle down. I guess Jimmy decided to give us the property to settle on because shortly after he passed I was notified by an attorney that Jimmy had left me some land on Madrona Island."

"And when was that?" I asked.

Banjo shrugged. "'Bout ten years ago."

"And you never visited the island until you moved here?"

"No. Didn't see the need. It's not like the land was going anywhere. Summer and I figured we'd check it out when we were ready to settle down, and if we liked it we'd stay and if we didn't we'd move on."

"Did either the attorney or Jimmy mention exactly how many acres you inherited?"

"Don't rightly remember. I think I have some paperwork at the house. I suppose I could look for it if it's important."

"That would help."

"Come by tomorrow and I'll give you what I have."

"Will you be here?"

"Guessin' that depends on what the day brings."

"Okay, I'll find you. And thanks."

I was heading back toward Coffee Cat Books to lock up when I saw a cat that looked a lot like Alice dart around the corner. I immediately changed direction and followed the flash of white, which stayed just far enough in front of me that I had no chance to catch her. When she turned the corner from Main Street onto Harbor Boulevard I began to jog. When she stopped and sat on the sidewalk in front of the old newspaper building I slowed to a walk and approached her slowly so as not to scare her off.

"What are you doing all the way over here?" I asked as I inched forward.

Alice watched me until I was just feet away from her, then scampered around the building. I called after her as I followed. She waited until I was almost close enough to grab her and then darted into a small opening that had been cut into the space below the floor for ventilation. There was no way I was going to be able to go in after her. I was contemplating what to do when I heard meowing coming from the front of the building. I went back to the sidewalk and looked in through the front window. Alice was sitting on the counter that had once been used as a reception desk.

"Come on, Alice," I said through the window. "I need to get back. I promised Tara."

Alice just looked at me.

"Ugh," I groaned.

I took out my cell and called Cody. "Do you still have a key to the newspaper?" I asked.

"Yeah. Orson said I could hang on to it until I made a decision about buying the place," Cody answered. "Why?"

"Alice has somehow gotten inside. She went in through the crawl space, but there must have been an opening into the building. She's refusing to come out."

"I'll be right there," Cody promised.

"I have to run back to Coffee Cat Books to lock up. I promised Tara I would. I have a feeling Alice wants us to check out something inside the building, so I'm betting she'll stay put until you get there."

"Okay. Come back to the newspaper building when you're done there."

By the time I got to Coffee Cat Books everyone was gone except for one man, who'd been kind enough to wait for me. I thanked him, locked up, and then headed back to the newspaper office. Cody was just pulling up out front as I jogged up. Luckily, Alice was still sitting on the counter, waiting for us.

"Where's Max?" I asked.

"I left him with Mr. Parsons and Francine. You can stop by to get him when we're finished here."

"Francine is with Mr. Parsons?"

"I didn't want to leave him alone. I called Banjo, but he didn't answer, and Maggie was still at the Bait and Stitch, so I called Francine. She said she'd come over to sit with him. She even brought a casserole she planned to heat up for dinner."

"That was nice of her."

"She said she was happy to do it. If you ask me, I think she's lonely. She lives alone with only her cats for companionship. She suggested that I should take you to dinner as long as we were out."

"Dinner?" I laughed. "Is she playing matchmaker?"

"No, I think she planned to watch a movie with Mr. Parsons and didn't want me underfoot. So how about it? I've been dying for a good pizza."

I shrugged. "I could eat. Let's see what's on Alice's mind first."

Cody unlocked the door and we walked in through the front door. Alice jumped off the counter and meowed as if to scold us for taking so long.

"Okay, you silly cat, why have you brought me here?" I asked.

Alice trotted down the hall and sat in front of a door that had the word MORGUE painted on the front.

"Don't worry," Cody said as he opened the door. "It's just where Orson kept old copies of the paper."

Alice seemed to know exactly where she was going. She trotted over to a shelf and sat down in front of it.

The particular shelf Alice led us to was piled with newspapers that were between three and five years old. There was one paper published each week, plus an annual anniversary edition, so there must have been over 150 issues on the shelf. I looked at Alice. "Any idea which one we're looking for?"

I swear, if cats could roll their eyes Alice would have rolled hers. She looked at me in such a way as to convey that she had gotten us this far and the rest was up to us. Cody and I each took a stack of newspapers and began to look through them. We had no idea what we were looking for, but I figured we'd know it when we found it.

Alice jumped up onto the table and began to purr. She seemed content with our efforts, so I imagined we were on the right track. Cody and I sat side by side as we began with the first issue of the year and thumbed through each newspaper, looking for anything that might seem relevant to Bill Powell's project, the land ownership discrepancy, or Mrs. Trexler's murder. It was fun, too, to revisit some of the events of the past few years.

"Didn't Orson have all this computerized?" I asked. "If he did we could just do a search for key topics."

Cody shook his head. "As I indicated before, Orson was stuck in the past. The very *distant* past. I'd be willing to bet that the *Madrona Island News* was one of the last newspapers still being printed on a press from the sixties."

"Yeah, I guess. Still, I miss having a paper dedicated to local news. If you decide not to buy it I hope someone else does."

"Actually, I'm planning to submit an offer to Orson tomorrow. If everything works out as planned I should be up and running before the end of the summer."

"You're going to have a huge job ahead of you if you want to turn this into a profitable venture," I warned.

"I've never been afraid of a challenge."

"Or a dare." I giggled as I recalled one particular dare, when I'd convinced Cody to attend the student council debates dressed in a cheerleader's uniform, makeup, and a wig. The dare had come at the conclusion of a discussion of stereotypes and the unlikelihood that anyone dressed in a cheerleader's uniform could actually win a debate.

"Which of the embarrassing dare-related events from my past are you referring to?" Cody moaned.

"The debate."

He smiled. "Yes, but I won that debate, disproving your theory in the process. I consider it one of my bigger victories."

"You had on a wig. A blond one."

Cody shrugged. "You might not know it, but I have a complexion that can pull off any hair color."

I almost fell on the floor laughing as Cody pretended to poof the hair on his shoulder.

"If I remember correctly there's is a photo of the cross-dressing Cody West in one of the newspapers in this room."

"As much as I would revel in taking a walk down memory lane, I think I found something." Cody shoved the newspaper he was looking at in front of me. "Look at this."

"Mrs. Sullivan's cat had kittens?" I asked, reading from a headline at the top of the page.

"No. Look at the small article at the bottom."

"'Land surveyed in anticipation of new development'?"

"That's the one," Cody confirmed.

"This says that the property Bill Powell purchased was surveyed a little over two years ago," I realized. "Bill purchased it a few months after that. It would be interesting to see whether the land Jimmy Lee left to Banjo and Summer was subdivided at that time."

"I'd be willing to bet we can get the survey report online. How about we just pick up a pizza and take it back to your cabin, where we can use the computer?"

"Sounds good to me." I looked at the cat. "Alice?"

Alice got up and pranced to the door. Apparently we'd found what it was she'd wanted us to see.

Cody locked up and then gave Alice and me a ride back to my car, which was parked in front of Coffee Cat Books. Then Alice and I got Max from Mr. Parsons's while Cody picked up the pizza. I'd had a late night the previous evening and I had a feeling I was in for another one.

Chapter 11

Friday, June 5

"Cody, wake up," I said, nudging the man who had fallen asleep on the sofa next to me. By the time we'd eaten our pizza, shared a bottle of wine, and searched the Web, trying to make sense of the information we'd uncovered, it had gotten pretty late. I don't remember falling asleep, but given the fact that we were both sacked out on my sofa, we must have.

"What time is it?" Cody yawned.

"Six-thirty. We must have fallen asleep."

"Mr. Parsons!" Cody jumped up. "I'm surprised Francine didn't call or come by to get me." He grabbed his shoes. "I should go. I'll call you later."

He gave me a quick peck on the cheek and headed for his car.

I looked at Max, who had his head tilted, as if he was trying to figure out what all the excitement was about.

"I have to say that wasn't how I imagined my first time spending the night with Cody would be."

Max barked.

"I'll change and we'll go for a run. I need to clear my head before I tackle Tara and the remodel."

It was a clear morning and looked as if it would be a beautiful day. I tried to focus on the beauty surrounding me, but all I could think about was the previous evening. I almost hated to admit it, but Cody and I made a good team. We seemed to think along the same lines and were quick to know how best to help the other with the answers we searched for. I was sorry the reason behind our impromptu sleepover was the death of a woman I had always liked and admired, but I was happy to realize that Cody and I had been able to rekindle our friendship without any lingering weirdness created by the memories of the night we'd shared ten years before.

As for the case of Maggie's poisoning and Mrs. Trexler's murder, I felt like we were narrowing in on an answer, but I wasn't sure exactly what that answer was. It appeared that Mrs. Trexler either tampered with Maggie's tea or was protecting the person who had. In either case she'd felt bad enough to go to Father Kilian to ask to make an emergency confession. He had felt it was important for her to confess what she knew to Maggie. When Mrs. Trexler refused an argument had ensued. Minutes later Mrs. Trexler was hit over the head with a heavy candlestick, which resulted in her death.

Mrs. Trexler had a journal in her home with clues leading to a plot of land. Orson had confirmed that she had written him asking for information about that land, which had turned out to be part of the property involved in Bill Powell's condo development. More specifically, the land was situated in the northernmost corner of the proposed development and appeared to have at one time been owned by Banjo, although he seemed to have no knowledge of the specifics of his inheritance. At the time Jimmy Lee purchased the land the ten acres had been intact. According to the guy at the assessor's office, the plot was likewise intact when Banjo inherited it. Banjo swore he didn't sell the land, nor did he give it away.

Bill Powell had ordered a survey two years ago, eight years after Banjo inherited it and several weeks before Bill purchased it. The reports that were generated as a result of the survey indicated that Tran Flanders owned the two acres Bill purchased.

When Banjo and Summer moved to Madrona Island eighteen months ago, land markers had been in place showing the boundaries of the property they inherited. They never stopped to question them. I hoped that when I caught up with Banjo today the paperwork he was provided with when he inherited the property would indicate the boundaries at the time of his inheritance. Of course the man at the survey office already had indicated that Banjo had inherited the full ten acres. It made sense that paperwork must exist somewhere that indicated when the two acres had been sectioned off.

Which brought me back to the larger issues in my mind: Who in the heck was Tran Flanders, and why was there no record of him?

As I turned inland to jog through the commercial section of Pelican Bay, I had to ask myself for the hundredth time how Banjo's land and Mrs. Trexler's involvement in Maggie's poisoning could possibly be related. Mrs. Trexler had been very outspoken in her opinion that the development shouldn't be approved. She seemed to have been doing research that in the very least had brought into light the possible discrepancy in the ownership of the land. Why would a woman who was working so hard to block the project be involved in the tampering of the tea of a woman who was likewise opposed to it?

I slowed my pace as I headed down Main Street. I was half-hoping Banjo had opened the store already, but I should have known he hadn't. The man wasn't one to get an early start to the day. Sometimes I admired the man's ability to go with the flow, taking life as it came. Not that I'm the uptight sort—at least not most of the time—but Banjo and Summer never seemed to sweat the small stuff and, most times, not even the big stuff either.

Cody and I had searched for documents that would prove the transfer of the land from Banjo to Tran Flanders the previous evening, but, despite the fact that we'd looked for hours, we'd been unable to find any indication that the land had ever been transferred at all.

I veered off Main Street and headed toward the home of Bella and Tansy. They never gave you an answer to your questions in an outright manner, but they did seem to have a knack for pointing you in the right direction.

Luckily, Bella was in her front yard puttering around with her roses, as she did most mornings. "Morning, Bella. Did your roses survive the storm?"

"I'm afraid the wind made quite a mess of them, but I'll have them back in shape in no time. The yellow roses on the north side of the house seem to have taken the brunt of the bad weather."

"I'm sure they'll rebound in no time at all."

"Yes, I'm sure they will." Bella put her pruning shears down on a bench. "I think I'll take a break and join you inside."

"I hate to interrupt your day."

"Nonsense. We've been expecting you."

Of course they had.

"Tansy has prepared tea and muffins."

I glanced at Max. "He's pretty sandy."

"That's perfectly fine. Tansy and I don't mind a little sand. How's Alice working out?"

"She's been very helpful, actually," I answered as I followed Bella up the walkway to the front door.

"It's good that you're close to wrapping things up. I'm afraid it's about time for Alice to return home."

"Close to wrapping things up?" I said as we walked in though the entryway and continued on toward the sunny kitchen. "I'm afraid we aren't anywhere near it."

"Of course you are. Sugar?"

I just looked at the woman.

"In your tea. Would you like sugar in your tea?"

"Oh. No. Black is fine."

Bella gave Max one of the dog treats she always seemed to have on hand even though she and Tansy didn't have a dog.

"Tansy will be down in a minute," Bella informed me. "Would you like a muffin?"

"Uh, sure."

Bella and I chatted about the weather and the upcoming Founders Day celebration while we waited for Tansy to make an appearance. Physically the two were as different as two women could be. Bella was tall and thin, with long blond hair that hung to her waist. Her fair skin was flawless and her eyes bluer than the ocean. Tansy, on the other hand, was small with dark hair and eyes. Both women seemed to possess some sort of heightened intuition, but Tansy was the most knowing of the pair by far.

"So what do you think of the muffins?" Tansy asked as she glided into the room on bare feet.

"They're really good."

"It's a new recipe I'm trying out. I thought you'd like them. Be sure to take some for Maggie when you go."

"I will. Thank you."

"It seems Tran is giving you a bit of a problem."

I must be getting used to talking to these strange women; I wasn't even surprised that Tansy knew it before I had a chance to ask her. "Yes. We found out he owns part of the land Banjo inherited, but we can't find any paperwork to show when the land was transferred, and we haven't been able to find any information about him either."

"Sometimes things become jumbled."

"Jumbled?"

"You have everything you need; you just have to look to know what to see."

"I don't suppose you can translate for me?" I looked at Bella.

"Sorry. Tansy is confident you'll work this all out. Sometimes it's good to call on old friends who might provide a new perspective."

"Thanks, I think. Max and I should be going."

"Until the next time." Tansy hugged me.

"What do you mean, jumbled?" Cody asked me later that morning after I'd picked up Haley and delivered her to Maggie. We were sitting at the table in Mr. Parsons's kitchen while he and Francine watched an old movie on television.

"I don't know. That's exactly what she said. She also said I should call on old friends to provide a new perspective."

"Like me?" Cody suggested.

I shrugged. "Maybe. I've known you my whole life, so I guess that would make you an old friend. I asked Tara, but she was completely distracted by her date last night."

"Tara went on a date?"

"New guy. He bought Shoreline Electric. According to Tara, he's the best thing to come along in forever."

Cody laughed. "I'm glad she found a nice guy. I always liked Tara."

"What if Tansy meant 'old' as in age when she said old friend?"

"Like Mr. Parsons?" Cody asked.

"It couldn't hurt to ask."

"I thought we weren't supposed to talk about this with anyone who didn't already know," Cody pointed out.

"That's true. I'll be glad when I don't have to keep this a secret any longer. It doesn't feel right to lie to people I know and love."

"It won't be much longer. Finn told me that he's going to have Father Kilian announce that Mrs. Trexler has passed without going into detail at the Sunday service. I think it's going to raise a lot of questions, but it has been a week. We can't sit on this forever."

"I can't believe that in a week's time no one has come around asking where she's been. She has friends."

"True, but remember, there's been a rumor going around that she's away on a trip. Does Mrs. Trexler have any children?" he asked.

"No. Finn looked for next of kin, but there really aren't any. It seems her husband left her for another woman when they'd only been married a short time. They never had children and she never remarried."

"And the ex?"

"He's since passed. Mrs. Trexler was an only child and her parents passed away years ago. He was trying to look into cousins and that sort of thing, but as of the last time we spoke he hadn't had any luck."

"Do you find it odd that Mrs. Trexler continued to be referred to as *Mrs.* Trexler even though her husband left her so early in their marriage?"

"I guess. I hadn't really thought about it, but I suppose it does seem odd. It's not like they had children together."

"I'm going to make some coffee. Would you like some?" Cody asked.

I nodded and picked up a copy of the newspaper that was on the corner of the table while Cody went to fill the coffeepot. It was a national paper so it didn't contain local news, but I supposed Mr. Parsons enjoyed reading about current events.

"Did you make your offer to Orson?" I asked.

"I did. He seemed interested. I think we might be able to work something out."

"So you're going to take Mr. Parsons up on his offer to move in on a permanent basis?"

"I'm seriously considering it. Did you know there's a back stairway? Living up on the third floor would be a lot like having my own apartment. The top floor is over three thousand square feet, which is bigger than many houses. If I put a little money into it I could add a kitchen, although I think Mr. Parsons would appreciate the company at mealtime."

"I can just picture the two of you sitting at this table in the morning, drinking your coffee and doing the daily jumble," I teased.

"Daily jumble," Cody mused. "I wonder if that's what Tansy meant when she said things were jumbled."

I frowned. "I guess it could be. But what exactly is jumbled? We figured out that the letters in the journal said sold/surveyed/transferred. I don't see how that's jumbled."

Cody scrunched up his face. "Yeah, that seems fairly obvious. I suppose she's referring to the property being sold to Jimmy Lee. We know it was surveyed two years ago. The records must have been updated at that point. The new records already show Tran Flanders as being the owner, so any transfer would have taken place before that. It seems like Mrs. Trexler's words are out of order. Based on what we know, it should read 'sold/transferred/surveyed.'"

"Yeah." I sighed. "I feel like there's a clue in the puzzle. If there wasn't, why would Mrs. Trexler even have written the stuff down?"

"Maybe Tara was wrong and the words don't say sold/surveyed/transferred after all. Maybe the letters were jumbled and she just didn't realize it."

I wrote the letters on the blank edge of the newspaper. It seemed that Tara's interpretation made sense. "Maybe we should ask Mr. Parsons if he sees anything different," I suggested. "He does these puzzles all the time. We don't have to tell him where we got the letters, or that Mrs. Trexler has been murdered."

Cody shrugged. "I guess it couldn't hurt to ask."

He and I took the paper and went into the living area where Mr. Parsons, Francine, Rambler, and Max were all watching a Doris Day movie. We explained that we wanted him to look at something to see what he thought of it. I had transferred the letters in their original format to the same newspaper page I had been messing around with.

"Looks like sold/surveyed/transferred," he said.

"Are you sure?" I asked.

He shrugged. "Seems to go with the key."

"What key?" I asked.

"Land transferred." He pointed to where I had written *Tran Flanders*.

"Of course," I realized. "The reason we can't find any information on Tran Flanders is because Tran Flanders doesn't exist."

"Then who owns the land?" Cody asked.

"What land?" Francine asked.

I looked at Cody. We'd promised not to tell anyone that Mrs. Trexler had been murdered, but we'd never agreed not to talk to anyone about the clues we'd found in the journal. Cody and I spent the next thirty minutes explaining, while remaining intentionally vague about the source of the clues.

"If the land had been sold there would be a record of it not only in the county records but in the newspaper," Mr. Parsons said.

Mr. Parsons was correct. Prior to the paper closing, there had been an entire section dedicated to legal notices such as the transfer of property.

"So we just need to figure out when this transfer was supposed to have taken place and then go through the old newspapers to see if we can find a notice of the transfer," I concluded.

"Seems like it'll be like finding a needle in a haystack unless you can narrow it down," Francine added.

"We know the property was surveyed two years ago," I began. "What if Bill Powell wanted to buy Banjo's land but couldn't track him down? He did live pretty much off the grid. It had been years since Jimmy Lee had passed, and Banjo had never even come to take a look at the property. Bill knew that owning two acres would give him the water access he needed, so he decided to have the land ownership transferred to a fake person. He ordered the land to be surveyed and then paid off the surveyor to list Tran Flanders as the legal owner. Banjo wasn't around, and there was no one to know about it or complain, so he got away with it. He then bought the land all nice and legal, like from Tran. Banjo showed up, and because he had never seen the land he didn't pay any attention to the boundaries."

"That actually sounds feasible," Cody applauded.

"What Bill didn't count on was that Mrs. Trexler would realize that the boundaries were wrong," I added. "Bill Powell found out she'd been digging around and killed her."

"Sue Trexler is dead?" Francine and Mr. Parsons both said at the same moment.

Chapter 12

I met John as promised to deliver the kitten, and then Cody and I went over to the newspaper to make a feeble attempt at finding something that would point us in the right direction. The problem was that if our assumption was correct, and the land was never legally transferred, we'd never find an announcement. We didn't know exactly when the transfer should have occurred, so we didn't know at what point the lack of an announcement indicated that one had never taken place. It really was like looking for a needle in a haystack.

"Hey, look at this," I said, pointing to an old photograph that had been printed a couple of years back, when the high school had celebrated its fiftieth anniversary. "That's Maggie on the end."

"She looks so young," Cody commented.

"I think she was a sophomore, or maybe a junior, when the school was built. It says here that the photograph was taken of the cast of the first play held in the new theater." I looked at the photo more closely. It was so odd to see people I knew as senior citizens looking so young.

"That looks like Marley." Cody pointed to a girl on the far end of the lineup.

I looked at the key beneath the photo. "It is Marley." I trailed my finger from the figure on the far end toward the right. "Next to Marley is someone named Leonard King, then Ella Winters, Jason Robinson, Maggie, Donald Trexler, Susan Boyle, and Nora Fitzgerald." I looked up from the newspaper and met Cody's eyes. "I bet Donald Trexler was Mrs. Trexler's husband."

"Could be. I don't remember hearing of any other Trexlers on the island. I guess the family must have moved away at some point."

"He's cute. Don't you think he's cute?"

"Adorable."

I grinned. "It's just that Mrs. Trexler is so formal and stringent. I always imagined that the man she was married to for a short time would be sort of nerdy and needy."

"Nerdy and needy?"

"Yeah. Uptight and formal. This guy is a total babe, and it says he played the male lead in the production, so he probably was outgoing. I never thought to ask Maggie about Mrs. Trexler's husband. I guess I figured they hadn't known each other."

"Do you think Ella Winters is Ms. Winters from the church?" Cody asked.

I frowned. "It's hard to tell. If it is the same person, Ms. Winters has changed a lot. I mean, it's been fifty years, so they've all changed, but the girl in the photo looks happy and carefree, whereas Ms. Winters seems sort of ..." I paused as I searched for the right word.

"Acidic?" Cody supplied.

"Exactly. She's very organized and always on top of things, but I'm not sure I've ever seen her smile."

"I remember hearing that some guy did her wrong when she was young and she never got over it. I guess a broken heart can make you bitter."

"'Did her wrong'? You been reading romance novels?" I teased.

"Maybe." Cody grinned.

I realized that the particular issue of the newspaper I was looking at was dedicated almost entirely to the school's anniversary. As I turned the pages, I paused to look at the black-and-white photos from so very long ago.

"Oh, look. Maggie was a cheerleader." I chuckled. "I can't believe she never told me that."

Cody leaned over and looked at the photo. "I have to say, your aunt was quite the looker. I'm surprised she never married. She was obviously popular. She still is."

"She told me once that there was a boy a long time ago. It didn't work out and it broke her heart, so she decided to focus on other things. She said that before she knew it her youth had passed and she was beyond childbearing age. She didn't see the point in marrying, so she never did."

"Wow, this guy really must have done a number on her."

I shrugged. "I guess. To be honest, I never gave it much thought. Doesn't it seem odd to you that so many women of Maggie's generation ended up alone?"

Cody appeared to be thinking about it but didn't say anything.

"Look at the facts," I continued. "Maggie never married; Marley never married; Mrs. Trexler married, but her husband left her after a short time; Francine's husband died shortly after they were married; Ms. Winters never married. For an island this tiny, it seems like there were a lot of women who are about the same age who all knew each other as teens and went to the same high school and who all lived their lives without a spouse."

"I guess you have a point. It does seem odd, now that you mention it. I wonder if there's a similar correlation with the guys."

I bit my lip as I considered Cody's question. "I'm not sure. Mr. Parsons never married, but he's quite a bit older than Maggie. Other than that, no one comes to mind." I looked back down at the table. "I guess we should get back to work."

We'd just spent twenty minutes discussing one newspaper. At this rate, we were going to die of old age ourselves before we got through the stack in front of us.

"You take that pile and I'll take this one," Cody suggested.

"This is pointless," I said after another forty minutes had gone by.

"I think I have to agree. I did find one interesting bit of information," Cody informed me.

"And that is?" I asked.

"According to this article, Bill Powell was considering other sites for his project in the event that the one he ended up with didn't work out."

I paused to consider the ramifications of this piece of news.

"If he had chosen another site it would have saved us a lot of hassle, and Mrs. Trexler might still be alive," I concluded.

"True. I really don't know that there's anything to find here," Cody decided. "I think we have a good theory; I just don't know how we can prove it."

"You're right, and I promised Maggie that I'd help her with the Founders Day float the Bait and

Stitch plans to enter in the merchants' competition. I should get going anyway."

"I'm going to stay to look through these papers a little more; you go ahead and take care of what you need to."

"Okay. Thanks. Let me know if you find anything."

"If I don't talk to you before then, good luck tomorrow."

"Thanks, but the float is really Maggie's baby. It's going to be awesome, though. You'll be there?"

"I wouldn't miss it."

As I left the paper, I tried to soak up the excitement the rest of the island seemed to be feeling. The parade was to be held the following morning, directly after the pancake breakfast. As I drove through Pelican Bay, I couldn't help but feel a sense of contentment in spite of the circumstances. One of the things I love most about Madrona Island is that the residents really know how to celebrate a holiday, no matter how large or small.

The festivities were set to kick off later that evening with a spaghetti dinner in the community center, followed by a play put on by the community theater. I'd thought of trying out this year, but the auditions had been held when Maggie had been at her worst, so I'd felt that staying home and taking care of her was more important.

The large baskets of flowers that hung from every lamppost on Main Street accentuated the blue and white decorations most merchants displayed in honor of the island's founding fathers. Founders Day was a popular event that promised to bring in droves of visitors from the mainland, as well as from the other islands in the area. Given the fact that it fell in early June, it doubled as a kickoff-to-summer fling as well.

My favorite part of the long weekend was the community picnic that was held in the park on Sunday afternoon. Everyone brought a dish to share, so the selection of delicious food was expansive. In addition to the wonderful food, there was an annual softball game between the parishioners of St. Patrick's and Madrona Island Community Church. I usually played for the Pats, although most years the Angels ended up winning. Of course Cody was home now, so this year the Pats had a better chance of winning than we'd had for a very long time.

In addition to helping Maggie finish her float I also still needed to figure out what type of potluck dish I was bringing to the picnic. It would have to be something easy because I still had to shop for the ingredients and then make it. I knew I wouldn't have time to do much in the way of menu planning today, but maybe tomorrow, between the fishing derby and the street dance.

I decided to stop by Ship Wreck in the hope that Banjo had opened, so we could have a quick chat before I headed over to the Bait and Stitch. Luckily, he was there, and the store wasn't busy.

"Found the paperwork you were looking for," Banjo said from behind the teak counter. Today his long gray hair was braided down the back and he was wearing one of the tie-dyed T-shirts Summer made over his faded blue jeans.

He handed me an envelope with the deed to the property, a copy of Jimmy Lee's will, and a map of the land he had inherited. It clearly showed that Banjo had inherited all ten acres from Jimmy Lee.

"And you're sure you never signed any other papers regarding the property?" I asked. It occurred to me that Banjo could have signed away the rights to the two acres without realizing what he was agreeing to.

"I'm sure. Don't see how this Tran person ended up owning part of my land when I didn't sell it to him."

"I have a theory," I said, and outlined the assumption Cody and I were currently working with.

"Guess it could have happened that way," Banjo agreed. "How can I help?"

"I'm not sure yet. I need to check on a few things and then I'll let you know. Are you entering a float in the parade this year?"

"Yeah. Summer rounded up some high school students to work on it. It's not going to be elaborate, but at least Ship Wreck will have a presence. You and Tara doing anything for Coffee Cat Books?"

"Not this year. We're still working on the remodel. But next year for sure. This year I'm helping Maggie."

"I had a chat with her earlier this morning. Seems like she's doing better."

"Yes, thankfully. She's almost back to her old self. I even heard her talking about trying to set up a debate before the election."

"Seems like folks mostly know who stands for what already," Banjo commented.

"I have to agree, but I guess Maggie thinks having everyone answer the same set of questions will help anyone who's on the fence make a decision. Personally, I hate to see her overdo it, but you know

Maggie. She's not one to be kept down. I should get going. Good luck in the parade."

"Good luck to you as well." Banjo waved as I exited his store, only to fall flat on my backside as a group of kids chasing a dog ran into me.

"Need some help?"

"Cam!" I smiled as I lifted my hand so he could help pull me to my feet. "I thought you'd left the area."

"I quit my job at the bank and plan to take my mom and sister on a trip, but we haven't left yet. I think my sister is feeling conflicted about leaving, but I'm afraid if she doesn't get away for a few weeks she's going to have a nervous breakdown."

I noticed that Cam looked tired. His eyes had lost their shine, and it looked like he'd lost quite a bit of weight. It had only been a little over a week since I'd seen him, but he looked like a totally different man.

"This must be really hard on her, and on you as well. I can't imagine what went through your mind when you realized who the guilty party was."

"To be honest, I momentarily considered keeping my mouth shut, but in the end I knew I couldn't do it. My brother-in-law invested almost all of his savings in Bill's project. I'm not sure what my sister is going to do if it doesn't get approved."

"Seems like a lot of people have a lot of good reasons for wanting the project to get approved, but just as many have really good ones for wanting it to be rejected."

"Guess that's the way it is with things like this. Some win and some lose."

"Yeah, I guess. Are you here for Founders Day?"

"Actually, I came by to pick up some stuff I'd left at the bank, but now that I'm here I'm thinking I might stay. I was chatting with one of the tellers, and she mentioned how much fun the weekend was. I could really use some fun."

I told him about the dinner and the play. "It's always a good time. You should come."

"Will you be there?"

I nodded.

"Okay then; if you'll attend the dinner and play with me maybe I'll stick around."

"I'd like that," I found myself saying, despite the fact that it would be unwise to get any more involved with a man who was about to leave the area, maybe for good.

"Wonderful. Do you want me to pick you up or do you want to meet at the dinner?"

"Let's meet there. I'm on my way over to help Maggie."

"I hear there's a street dance tomorrow night," he continued.

"They close Main Street to vehicles and set up food vendors and a live band. It's really a lot of fun. They have a new band this year that I hear is excellent. Even if you don't feel like dancing, they should be good to listen to. Are you staying in town?"

"I'm staying at Francine's tonight and then I guess I'll see."

"Didn't you tell me a while back that Francine was having a Founders Day party?"

"She was going to, but with everything that has happened in the past couple of weeks she decided to cancel it."

"Did she tell you that she decided to adopt Romeo?"

"No." Cam looked as shocked as I'd been when she asked me about it. "I haven't been over to her place yet. It'll be good to see the big guy. I can't believe that after all the trouble we went through trying to keep the cats apart she ended up adopting him."

"I guess under her oftentimes gruff exterior Francine believes in true love."

I chatted with Cam for a few more minutes and then continued down the street. When I walked around the alley to the Bait and Stitch I almost turned around and went back out the way I'd come. The place was packed with the volunteers who had shown up to help with the float. Even Tara had taken a day off from the remodel to do her part.

"Wow! You've gotten so much done already."

"It looks great, doesn't it?" Maggie beamed.

"It really does. The cats in the boat are adorable. I especially love the one that's sewing."

"I figured we could advertise the Bait and Stitch *and* give Harthaven Cat Sanctuary a plug."

"Do you like the float?" Haley called down from the bed of the flatbed truck.

"It looks wonderful."

Haley hopped down and hugged me. "I'm having so much fun. Maggie said I could ride on the float in the parade."

"That's great. Will your aunt be there to see you?"

Haley's smile faded. "No. She had to go to Seattle this weekend, so she's going to miss everything. But," she grinned, "she said I could stay with Maggie for the whole weekend and Maggie said it was okay.

We're going to the dinner tonight and then the play, and tomorrow is the pancake breakfast, the parade, and the dance. I'm superexcited."

"Me too." I hugged the enthusiastic little girl.

"Are you going to help us with the float?" Haley asked.

I hesitated. I really did want to go home and get cleaned up before my date with Cam.

Maggie looked around. "I'd say we have enough help if you have something else to do. Are you planning on going to the dinner tonight?"

"I am. Cam is in town and I'm going with him."

"Haley and I are going to head directly over there when we're done here. I told the committee we'd help prepare the food. By the way, Doris was by earlier. She hoped you'd be here. She said she had some news you might be interested in."

"Did she say what the news might be?"

"No, and I didn't want to probe. You know how Doris likes to go on and on. I had a float to build and didn't want to get into some long conversation. I did see her chatting with Marley, though, so you can ask her if she knows what was on Doris's mind."

"I'll do that and see you both at the dinner. And I'll tend to the cats, so you don't have to worry about them tonight."

Marley didn't know what Doris wanted to speak to me about, but she did say she'd been on her way to the community center to get started on the sauce for the spaghetti. I decided it wouldn't really be out of my way to stop there before heading home.

The first thing I noticed when I walked through the front door of the building was the wonderful aroma of tomatoes and garlic.

"Maggie said you were looking for me," I told Doris, who was slicing mushrooms.

She nodded. "I know you've been looking for the person who tampered with Maggie's tea, and I thought you should know that Patience Tillman has been bad mouthing your aunt all over town. Apparently, Patience is convinced that her husband has eyes for Maggie."

I'd heard that before from Marley, but I didn't see Patience as the type to poison someone, even if she was jealous of her.

"I appreciate your telling me this, but I doubt Patience would poison Maggie over what has to amount to nothing more than gossip."

"I wouldn't be too sure. I'm in the Bait and Stitch a lot, and I can tell you that Toby tends to hang around whenever Maggie's there. He claims he needs to buy fishing supplies, but he draws each visit out and he's gone out of his way to do little things for Maggie ever since she's been sick. Some might say he's just being a good neighbor, but I can see why Patience would be upset."

"I appreciate your sharing this with me. Maybe I'll have a chat with Patience just to make sure everything is okay."

"Best be prepared for an earful. That woman isn't happy about the situation, and she's not afraid to let everyone know it."

Chapter 13

The community center was packed with islanders of all ages, sharing a meal and catching up on the local gossip. I'd taken more time than I'd planned with my appearance and so was later than I'd expected to be. Cam had already arrived and was sitting at a table with Tara, a man I assumed must be Carl, Finn, and Haley. Danny was sitting at a table with Melanie and some of her friends. I didn't see Maggie, but if I had to guess I'd say she was helping out in the kitchen. I looked around for Cody, but he didn't appear to be in the building. It made sense that he would have stayed home with Mr. Parsons; Francine was serving the pasta and Banjo and Summer were hanging out with friends at a table in the back of the room.

Cam and Tara scooted apart on the cafeteria bench when I joined them.

"You look nice," Haley complimented me.

"You really do," Tara agreed. "Is that a new dress?"

"Not really," I lied. I realized that it might have been a tactical error to take so much time with my appearance because it's something I rarely do. If people continued to make comments Cam would know that I'd dressed up for him, and I wasn't certain that was a message I wanted to send.

"Guess I didn't realize little Caitlin Hart was all grown up," Finn teased.

I kicked him under the table. Hard.

"Maggie is going to take me to buy a new dress for the dance tomorrow night." Haley saved me by changing the focus of the conversation.

"That's wonderful. Do you have a color in mind?" I asked.

"I was thinking blue, but your red dress looks so nice, I might look for red."

"I saw a dress in the window of Harbor Casuals that looked like it might fit you," I responded. "It was a deep emerald green that would match your eyes. I bet if we curled all that beautiful brown hair you'd look like Cinderella."

"Would you help me?" Haley asked. "With the hair?"

"I'd be happy to."

"I saw a picture of my mom when she was younger and she had her hair curled in long ringlets. Maybe we can do something like that."

I reached out and took a lock of Haley's hair in my hand. "I think that would be just perfect."

"Aren't you going to eat?" Haley asked when she realized I'd never filled a plate.

I wanted to say yes because I was starving, but knowing my luck when I was around Cam, I'd probably end up with the entire plate of spaghetti in my lap. "I'm not really all that hungry," I answered, just to be safe.

I watched as Patience Tillman walked into the room and got into line. "On second thought, maybe I will have a small plate. Save my place."

I hurried across the room before someone else got behind Patience, which was unwise, considering I had on the high heels I'd purchased with the dress but had never worn. I'm much more of a tennis shoes or flip-flops sort of gal, so hurrying anywhere in heels wasn't really a good idea. With my luck, I was going to slip on the freshly waxed floor and break my coccyx.

"Looks like a good turnout," I opened casually.

"Yes, I suppose it is."

"Is Toby with you?"

Patience scowled. "He's in the kitchen, helping out."

"That's nice. I didn't realize he was on the committee."

"He isn't."

Yikes. I could see where this was heading.

"I'm sure the committee is grateful for his help," I tried.

"Yes, I'm sure they are. I see Maggie is back to her old self."

"She's doing much better." I scooted forward as the line moved.

"I noticed she's in charge of the garlic bread again this year. Seems like she'd be too worn out to stand over a hot oven for so long."

"You know Maggie. She's not one to stay down long." I piled a large helping of salad onto my plate. Salad seemed safer than spaghetti, given the fact that I had to make my way back across the floor in the heels, which were killing me already. "Since Toby is helping Maggie in the kitchen you're welcome to join us at our table if you'd like," I offered politely.

"Thank you, but Doris is saving me a place at her table. It was good talking to you."

I watched Patience walk away. Maybe Doris hadn't been all that far off about her anger about the attention her husband was paying to Maggie. She certainly seemed upset about his desertion to the kitchen. The question was, was she upset enough to make Maggie sick? I hated to think that was the case. I carefully made my way back across the floor to the table without spilling a single piece of lettuce.

My sister Cassie came in with some of her friends just as I sat down between Tara and Cam.

"Hey, Cassie," I greeted. "I'd like you to meet Haley. She's working for Maggie and me helping out at the sanctuary for the summer."

I prayed *nice* Cassie and not *nasty* Cassie had shown up tonight. It seemed that lately you could never be sure who was lurking behind her blue eyes.

"Hi, Haley. It's nice to meet you," Cassie responded. "If you get tired of hanging out at the geriatric table you can join my friends and me."

Haley looked uncertain.

"Go ahead. If you're going to be here for the whole summer it will be good if you make some friends closer to your own age."

"Love the dress," Cassie said to me.

"Thank you." I prayed Cassie would leave it at that and not make a comment about trying to impress the babe sitting next to me.

Cassie looped her arm through Haley's. She gave me a silent look that communicated her intention to take care of her. I shot her a silent look of thanks.

"You're going to love my friends," she said to Haley as they started across the room.

I let out a deep sigh of relief.

"Everything okay?" Cam asked.

"Yeah. Everything is great."

By the time I got home I was both exhausted and agitated. The dinner had been a success. Cassie and Haley had gotten along like old friends, my mother hadn't embarrassed me in front of Cam, Carl had seemed nice, and Tara had seemed happy. To top it all off, Finn and Cam had gotten along better than I'd hoped, considering that they'd met under trying circumstances, and Maggie had been enthusiastic and energetic. I should be feeling content and settled rather than restless and worried.

I let Max out for a quick run while I fed Alice. It was late, and I had to be at the pancake breakfast early. I knew I should go directly to bed, but instead I found myself tossing a match on the fire and pouring myself a glass of wine. Then I changed into my jammies and curled up on the sofa. I clicked on the television even though there wasn't anything on I wanted to watch.

Max jumped up onto the sofa next to me and Alice climbed into my lap. It was a perfect end to a perfect evening. I really didn't know what my problem was. Cam had been sweet and attentive and the play was funny and lighthearted, but my mind kept wandering to land grabs, murder suspects, and Cody.

I buried my face in Alice's soft fur. The last thing I needed was to fall in love with Cody. Again. I'd been there. I'd moved past it. I knew that all we were meant to be were friends. Good friends. Friends who shouldn't risk what they had for what they might never have. For the first time I realized that Tara and I were in the same boat. We were both in love with seemingly unobtainable guys. Not that they couldn't be persuaded to enter the realm of intimacy; I'd certainly proved that in the past. But experience had shown that bringing intimacy into a friendship put it at risk.

I thought about Tara and Danny, mostly because it was easier to think about their ill-fated relationship than Cody and mine. I could have sworn that any infatuation between them was completely one-sided, but tonight, as Tara had enjoyed her evening with Carl and Danny had been tied up with Melanie, I was willing to swear I'd noticed him noticing her with a look that said so much more.

I remembered Cody telling me that my feelings for him when we were in high school hadn't been one-sided. I hadn't believed him at the time. I'd just figured he was trying to make me feel better about making such a huge fool of myself. Still, maybe . . .

I realized that thinking about Cody and what there might or might not have been between us in the past and what there could or couldn't still be between us was making me crazy. It was better to think about something less conflicted, like catching the monster who'd killed Mrs. Trexler and poisoned Maggie.

"So what do you think?" I asked Alice. So far the cat had done more to solve the murder than anyone else. "Did Bill Powell kill Mrs. Trexler?"

Alice yawned.

"Did Bill Powell poison Maggie?"

Alice lay down and rolled over onto her back.

"Did Bill Powell steal Banjo's land?"

Alice got up and walked across the room and knocked Mrs. Trexler's journal, which I had left on the kitchen table, onto the floor. I got up and picked it up, then brought it back to the sofa and opened it. I'd looked at the journal a million times already, so I didn't know what Alice thought I'd see this time that I hadn't seen before. We'd already figured out that the numbers she'd written down corresponded to the coordinates of the land Jimmy left to Banjo. We'd already figured out that Tran Flanders was an anagram for land transfer, not the name of some unknown person. It appeared the letters in the journal were simply the words sold/surveyed/transferred written backward. There really wasn't much else to find as far as I was concerned. Still, I knew Alice wouldn't be staring at me with a look of impatience if there was nothing more to find.

"This would be a lot easier if you would learn to talk."

"Meow."

"Human talk, not cat talk," I clarified.

Alice lay down and began to purr. It appeared she had more confidence in my ability to figure this out than I did.

Maybe I was going about this all wrong. I was trying to figure out who would steal Banjo's land *and* kill Mrs. Trexler *and* poison Maggie. When Keith Weaver had been murdered assuming that one person had killed Keith Weaver *and* bribed Gary Pixley *and* poisoned Maggie had caused me to keep my suspect list too narrow, which had led me to almost miss the answer to all three questions. If that was true again, maybe I needed to focus on one problem at a time.

As far as the illegal acquisition of Banjo's land went, on the surface it seemed only Bill Powell had anything to gain. But that wasn't really true. If Bill, after realizing he wasn't able to buy the piece of land that was key to making the project feasible, decided he'd move the project elsewhere, the landowners who were on the verge of making a huge profit by selling to him would be out a pretty penny. I knew that land had changed hands a few times, but in the end there were only two landowners involved—Nora Bradley and Tim Davenport. The land Nora owned had been in her family for generations, but Tim had bought the land much more recently, just prior to the survey.

I got up to retrieve the papers I'd had copied from the file in the county office from my backpack. Tim had bought ten acres from Mrs. Trexler's father long before Bill Powell came on the scene, but he'd also bought ten acres from Grover Cloverdale three years ago, which was just about the time Bill first came to the island. What if Tim, who was a Realtor, knew he was looking to build there, so he bought the land from Grover in anticipation of selling to Bill? He'd have a significant investment in the project, an investment that would be worthless if Bill moved the project to another location.

"It had to be Tim who ordered the survey and stole the land," I said aloud.

Alice got up and licked me on the face.

"I have to call Cody." I looked at the clock. "No, I can't call Cody. It's much too late. Besides, I'm not sure there's anything we can do to prove it tonight."

Alice just looked at me.

"We need to see if we can find out who surveyed the land. Once we track that person down we can find out who bribed them to alter the map."

Chapter 14

Saturday June 6

It seemed I had barely closed my eyes before my alarm was blaring that it was time to get up. I rolled out of bed and stumbled into the kitchen. Luckily, I had thought to set the timer on the pot, so there was hot coffee waiting to wake me up. I poured my first cup and downed it as quickly as I could without scalding the inside of my mouth, then poured a second before heading for the shower.

By the time I'd finished my third cup and dried and styled my hair I was feeling almost human. I had promised to help out at the pancake breakfast, but I decided it wouldn't be the end of the world if I called Cody first, even if it made me a few minutes late. After I explained my new theory of who might have created Tran Flanders, he promised to go online to see what he could find and then call me back with the results.

As I rode my bike into town, I tried to let myself get caught up in the hyperactive mood of the town. Pretty much everyone who lived on the island was descending on the community center for pancakes before lining up along the main road for the parade. I'd always loved Founders Day when I was a little girl. I can remember waking up early and hurrying to dress so we could get a prime spot along the parade route. For most of my growing-up years my older siblings had participated in the parade in one way or another. I was always considered to be too young to participate, so when I was in the seventh grade I joined the marching band at the middle school just so I could take part in the annual event. To this day I can't play the clarinet, but marching in my perfectly pressed uniform on those early June days as hundreds of people clapped and cheered is still one of my fondest memories.

Once I arrived at the breakfast I was assigned the duty of helping to serve the food. As far as I was concerned, serving was the primo job assignment. You got to chat with everyone who came through the line for a minute, and unless you were a real klutz you didn't get covered in food like you did either working in the kitchen or helping with the cleanup.

"Good morning, Father Kilian, Sister Mary. Would you like some eggs?"

Both of them nodded.

"I'm so happy to see such a wonderful turnout," Sister Mary commented. "It warms my heart when neighbors come together to share a meal."

"It does seem like everyone made the effort this year," I agreed.

I know this is going to sound strange, but I found myself wanting to avoid Father Kilian's eye. It seemed odd that we shared this huge secret, while even Sister Mary hadn't been filled in on the most recent events.

"Are you both coming to the picnic tomorrow?" I asked the pair, although I continued to make eye contact only with Sister Mary.

"We wouldn't miss it," Sister Mary answered for both of them. While she looked as serene as always, I could see the stress lines around Father Kilian's mouth.

"We're running low on sausages, if you don't mind fetching some from the back," Doris told me.

"I'm on it," I responded. "It was nice chatting with you," I said to the priest and nun as I turned toward the kitchen.

I was glad Father Kilian was finally going to announce to the congregation that Mrs. Trexler had passed during services the next day, but I did worry about what the announcement would mean for the picnic.

"We need more sausages," I said to Tara, who was working in the kitchen, covered in a thin film of flour and grease.

"I just fried up the last of it. Hopefully, most of the people who plan to eat have done so already."

"It's thinning out a bit," I informed her. "The parade starts in half an hour. I was late getting into town, so I didn't have time to stop off at the Bait and Stitch. How did the float turn out?"

"It's adorable," Tara said, confirming what I already suspected. "And Haley is so excited to ride on it. I can't remember the last time I saw *anyone* that excited about *anything*."

"I forgot to bring my camera, so the one on my phone will have to do. Are you going to the fishing derby this afternoon?" I asked.

Tara sighed. "I volunteered to help with the scales. I'm not sure why I signed up for so many events. I'm pretty much occupied all day and into the evening. How about you? Are you going to the derby?"

I looked around the room. It was crowded but loud, and no one seemed to be listening to us. I lowered my voice. "I came across some information last night that Cody is looking into as we speak. If it pans out we plan to go talk to Finn, so we might miss the derby."

"What kind of information?" Tara whispered back.

"I'll tell you later."

My phone beeped, informing me that I had a text. It was from Cody, and he'd found something. He'd called Finn and they planned to meet at his office.

"I have to go," I told Tara.

"Go ahead and do what you need to do. We're almost done here anyway. But hurry. You won't want to miss the parade."

I literally ran over to Finn's office on Second Street, arriving just as Cody was getting out of his truck.

"If I knew you didn't have your car I could have stopped by to pick you up," Cody said.

"I rode my bike into town." I took several deep breaths in an effort to slow my heart rate.

"So why didn't you ride it over here?"

"I forgot I had it until I was halfway here."

Cody raised one eyebrow.

"I tend to act first and think later. You know that. You said to meet you and I took off running."

Cody laughed. He put an arm around my shoulder. "You're really something, Caitlin Hart."

I wasn't sure if he meant that in a good way or a bad one, but I decided it was better not to ask.

"So what did you find?" I asked.

"Let's go inside and I can explain what I found to you and Finn at the same time."

After I'd called Cody he'd gone back to look at the copies of the maps that were attached to the links Orson had sent Mrs. Trexler. He'd realized that one of the links led to the map that was produced as a result of the survey. If my theory that the new map relocated the property lines to show that Tran Flanders owned the two acres Bill Powell needed was correct, the person who'd surveyed the land had been in on the land grab and would be able to identify who'd hired him.

When we were able to lay everything out for Finn, he agreed we had enough to bring the man in for questioning, which he promised us he would do. That left Cody and me free to head over to the parade.

"You know, if we're right, and Finn arrests Davenport, this whole thing is going to seem sort of anticlimactic," I commented.

"Personally, I prefer anticlimactic to you being in danger like the last time."

"Yeah, I guess. Is someone with Mr. Parsons?" I asked.

"Francine, Banjo, and Summer are bringing him to the parade. I was concerned about his leg getting jostled, but he really does need to get out of the house, and the three of them promised to create a virtual fortress around his wheelchair so no one runs into him."

"We can join them if you'd like."

Cody shrugged. "I thought that since Mr. Parsons is in good hands I'd take a break and maybe hang out with Danny. He said he was going to be at the far end of the parade route, near the marina. You're welcome to tag along, unless you have plans with Cam."

Did I detect a hint of jealousy in Cody's voice? I hadn't seen him the previous evening, but obviously someone had informed him about my date with Cam.

"I'd love to join you and Danny, but I think I'm going to check in with Maggie first to make sure she's all set. Besides, I want to wish Haley luck. I'll meet you over there when I'm done. If you decide to go somewhere other than the marina call or text me."

The sidewalks on both sides of the street were packed with people crammed into every available space along the parade route. They'd cordoned off the street, and there were volunteers walking the lines to make sure that all the spectators stayed behind them. That was probably a good idea from a safety standpoint but a total nightmare if you were trying to get somewhere. I decided it would be faster to go the long way around and enter the parade staging area from the alley. It was twice as far but half as crowded.

As I made my way around back, I noticed a blue sedan parked behind the Bait and Stitch. I was certain Maggie had told me they were going to be closed for the day so that everyone could attend the festivities. I decided it was my duty to check out the situation. You never knew when someone might take advantage of all the commotion to rob the place. I snuck in through the back door as quietly as I could. If there was a burglary in progress I'd scoot back to call Finn. On the other hand, if someone had just parked their car in the alley to avoid the crowd on the street I wouldn't be wasting his time.

The store was dark, but I hated to turn on any lights in case there really was a robbery in progress. The last thing I wanted to do was alert a thief to my presence.

I slowly made my way up the main aisle, looking down each side one as I passed. The area where the quilting table was located was open, with good visibility, but the fishing side of the store contained tall shelves that reached almost to the ceiling arranged in long aisles.

I felt my heart pounding as I slowly walked through the dark store. The fact that I couldn't see what was around each corner until I turned it created a level of tension I hoped mainly existed in my imagination. I was about to turn back toward the entrance when I heard a crash from the back of the store. I know that at this moment I should have scooted my way outside and called Finn, but you know me: impulsive. For some reason it seemed like a really good idea to first see *who* had broken in and *then* leave the way I had arrived.

I slowly crept down the dark aisle as silently as I could. I took a deep breath as I rounded the last corner, which would lead into the break room, where I suspected the perpetrator was located

I'm not sure what I expected to see or who I expected to find, but I would never in my wildest dreams have come up with the scene in front of me.

"It was you," I accused the person holding the tin in which Maggie kept her tea. "You poisoned Maggie and killed Mrs. Trexler. Why?"

Chapter 15

"What are you doing here?" the woman with the gun asked me. "I thought everyone was at the parade."

"I was on my way over to meet Danny when I saw your car. Why did you do it?"

"Magdalene seduced our men away from us. She pierced our souls and altered the natural course of our lives. She needed to be stopped before she could sin again."

"Are you nuts?" I really didn't have to ask that question because I could see it was true. I needed to get out of there. The woman had obviously gone over the edge. Way over. I suppose my best bet was to keep her talking until I could distract her enough to get the gun or at least get out. "Mrs. Trexler told Father Kilian she knew who was poisoning Maggie. She knew it was you, but for some reason she was protecting you. Why?"

Ms. Winters just stared at me. I could see she was trying to decide whether to give me the answer I'd asked for. She was a stern woman with a sour look that no amount of makeup could ever cover. Not that she wore makeup. In fact, the woman seemed to go out of her way to dress as nunlike as possible. I had to wonder why she hadn't joined a convent rather than working as housekeeper for Father Kilian her entire life.

"When I realized she was about to sin for a third time we knew we had to stop her," she finally answered.

"Sin for the third time? Sin with who?"

Ms. Winters didn't say anything, but suddenly I knew. "Toby Tillman. You thought that because Toby had been hanging around Maggie she was going to steal him from Patience. Is Patience in on this too?"

"Patience is a weak woman who doesn't know how to protect that which is hers."

"So you noticed Toby noticing Maggie and decided to intervene by making her sick. I have to assume you didn't intend to kill her because she didn't die. Mrs. Trexler developed a conscious and was on the verge of spilling the beans to Father Kilian, so you killed her. I should have realized you were the only other person who was around that night and could have done it."

"Father Kilian can't know that I have sinned."

I realized in that moment that she planned to kill me too. I didn't have enough time to come up with a logical argument as to why she shouldn't, so I decided to lie. I'd seen on a cop show that if you shared a confidence with someone and got them to share a confidence in return they'd trust you and be less likely to kill you.

"I can see that your heart is broken and your intention pure. I, too, have suffered the loss of a man to another woman. It can dig at your soul until it leaves nothing but a festering wound that eats away at your life just a little more every day." I hoped that was sappy enough to get her attention.

"So you do understand?" Ms. Winters lowered the gun just a bit.

"I understand that you felt you were doing the right thing. You were just trying to protect Patience from suffering the same agony you yourself have had to bear your entire life. I promise I won't tell anyone what you've done. I do, however, have a favor to ask."

"And what is that?"

"I'd like to know how Maggie hurt you and Mrs. Trexler. We share the same blood. If it's tainted I have the right to know."

I started to inch forward.

At first Ms. Winters didn't say anything. I feared she saw right through me. But then she began to speak. "I was in love once. I was young, and I believed that love was enough to forge an unbreakable bond between two people. I was so happy. So very, very happy, and then Jason fell under your aunt's hypnotic gaze and left me."

I remembered that the boy standing next to a much happier Ms. Winters in the photo in the newspaper had been named Jason.

"And Mrs. Trexler?" I asked.

"Her husband of only a year left her for another woman. Like myself, she bore the heartbreak for the rest of her life. When we noticed what was happening between Maggie and Toby we knew we needed to step in."

"You said Maggie was about to sin for the third time. Did Mrs. Trexler's husband leave her for Maggie?"

"No. I was referring to Maggie and Father Kilian."

What?

I could hear the parade passing by on the street. I realized that if Ms. Winters still planned to shoot me she'd use the noise provided by the marching band to do so. As plans went mine was lame, but a plan is still a plan.

"Oh my God, look behind you," I screamed.

She did, and I knocked the gun from her hand. For a moment I felt like an action hero, but then I realized the woman was seventy, nearsighted, and arthritic. I probably could have overpowered her at any time.

Later that evening I was sitting in my cabin in front of a roaring fire. I'd decided I'd had enough excitement for one day, so I'd decided to skip the dance. I did have a conversation with Camden before he left the island, though. I wished him well and encouraged him to stay in touch.

After I'd taken the gun from Ms. Winters I'd called Finn, who'd escorted her to the only jail in the area, which was located at Friday Harbor on San Juan Island. She'd have company that evening because he'd also arrested Tim Davenport after the man who'd surveyed FS6-P7confessed to accepting a bribe and altering the property map.

I wanted to ask Maggie about Ms. Winter's accusations, especially regarding Father Kilian, but she was busy with Founders Day events, and I hated to ruin her day. Haley was having the time of her life with Maggie, Marley, and Cassie, who were all dancing around the street like schoolgirls.

I was trying to decide whether to put on an old movie or just go up to bed when there was a knock on the door. I opened it to find Cody, alongside a woman about my age and a small child who looked to be four or five.

"Cody, what brings you here at this time of night?" I asked.

"This is Julia and her daughter, Alice. I met them while I was working one of the booths at the dance. It seems Alice has lost her cat, and I realized you might have found her."

"Have you found Snowball?" the little girl with huge brown eyes asked.

I frowned. "I have a lot of cats; can you describe her?"

"She's all white with a blue collar that says *Belongs to Alice.*"

I smiled. "Then, yes, I most certainly have found her."

I was going to miss Alice, whose name wasn't Alice after all, but when I saw how happy both cat and child were when they were reunited, I knew Snowball had only been on loan for a short time.

"Are you okay?" Cody asked after the woman and her daughter had left.

"Yeah, I'm okay. I knew Alice wasn't here to stay. I'm grateful the universe saw fit to lend her to us."

"She did seem to have a knack for knowing what needed to be done," Cody responded. "Are you planning to go back into town?"

"No. I'm much too tired to dance around in the street."

"Yeah," Cody agreed. "Me too."

"Would you like to watch a movie and share a bottle of wine?"

"I'd love to."

"Mr. Parsons?" I asked.

"Asleep. He had quite a big day. Banjo and Summer are at his place and plan to stay until I return."

Cody opened the wine while I looked for the glasses.

"So I heard you managed to solve the mystery of the tainted tea," Cody commented.

I shrugged. "I caught a break."

"Sounds like good instincts on your part. I could have used you on my squad in the Navy."

"If we were both in the Navy it would be *you* who would be on *my* squad," I teased.

"You know, I don't doubt that for a minute." Cody held up his glass. "I think we should toast."

"To what? My not getting shot when I tackled Ms. Winters?"

"Partially."

"So what else are we celebrating?" I asked as I sat down next to Cody, who was relaxing on the sofa.

"Orson accepted my offer and I officially informed the Navy of my intention to retire at the end of my leave."

"That's wonderful." I hugged the man sitting next to me. "When do you plan to start publishing?"

"I need to go back to finalize things with the Navy, and then I'll need to move the stuff I have in storage into Mr. Parsons's house, so I think I'm looking at the fall."

"Just in time for the annual harvest festival."

"I'd love to be able to cover the event, so I guess I'll make that my goal. I was talking to Tara's date, and it seems that a lot of the guys who are working on the bookstore will be able to hop over to help me with both the remodel to the newspaper office and the one to Mr. Parsons's third floor when they're finished working for you."

"I doubt our project will be done by September."

"That's not what I've heard. I chatted with several of the contractors while I was in town working the booth, and they say Tara has been riding them hard. They plan to wrap things up by the first of August. If they can take care of what I need done at the paper after that I should be ready to go to print by the time the harvest festival rolls around."

"Wow. That *is* soon. I don't know whether to be happy or terrified."

"Owning the shop is going to be a big step, but with Sergeant Tara on duty you should be fine. She really seems to know how to get things done."

"Yeah, she's great. I'm afraid I haven't been a very good partner so far. I really haven't helped at all."

"What you were doing was important. So now that all the current murders on Madrona Island have been solved, are you up to solving a not-so-current one?"

I frowned. "What are you talking about?"

Cody handed me a copy of a newspaper article that he'd been carrying in his pocket.

"While I was going through the old newspapers looking for information on Bill's project, I came across an article about a murder that occurred twenty-five years ago that was never solved."

I turned so that I was looking directly at Cody. "What sensational murder? I've lived here my entire life and don't remember anything about a sensational murder."

"Read the article," Cody instructed.

I began reading. "Oh—my—God." I looked up at him. "How could something like this even happen?"

"That's exactly what I hope to find out."

Grimm's Furry Tail

A Whales and Tails Mystery #3
Coming in March 2015

Cody discovers a previously unpublished edition of the newspaper he plans to buy that details a murder that occurred decades ago. The fact that the story was written but never published piques the curiosity of the friends, who decide to delve into a cold case that reaches back fifty years. When the truth is discovered they struggle with the ramifications of what they have uncovered. They know that revealing it will rock the small island community to its core.

Recipes for
The Mad Catter

Recipes by Kathi Daley:

Linguini and Broccoli
Pizza Casserole
Seafood Lasagna
Sloppy Joe Pasta

Recipes submitted by readers:

Cranberry Bread—submitted by Veronique Boudreau
Spaghetti Salad—submitted by Janel Flynn
Spaghetti and Meatballs—submitted by Maureen
Devlin-Murphy
Mike's Favorite Chicken Pot Pie Casserole—
submitted by Vivian Shane
Ricotta Cheese Chocolate Chip Cookies—submitted
by Bobby Toby
Coconut Lime Pie—submitted by Melissa Nicholson

Linguini and Broccoli

2 tbs. olive oil
2 cups broccoli, cut into small pieces
2 cloves garlic, minced
Pine nuts (I like a lot, but you can adjust quantity to taste)
1 cup white wine
1 pkg. linguini (1 lb.)
1 cup feta cheese
1 can sliced olives
Salt and pepper

Heat olive oil in a sauté pan. Sauté broccoli, garlic, and pine nuts until broccoli is tender. Add wine.

Cook linguini per directions on box. Drain. Toss with broccoli mixture, feta cheese, olives, salt, and pepper.

Pizza Casserole

1 lb. ground sausage (can use ground beef)
1 pkg. sliced pepperoni
2 jars pizza sauce
1 can sliced black olives
4 cups macaroni, cooked and drained
2 cups shredded mozzarella

Brown sausage, then add pepperoni, sauce, and olives.

Add to cooked and drained macaroni.

Place in large baking dish. Cover with cheese and bake at 350 degrees until cheese is bubbly.

I like to turn on the broiler for a few minutes so the cheese is browned.

Seafood Lasagna

Sauce:
1 cube butter
8 oz. cream cheese
1 cup heavy cream
Nutmeg
Salt
Pepper
1 cup grated Parmesan cheese
1 cup grated Romano cheese
1 cup sour cream
1 cup ricotta cheese
1 pkg. lasagna noodles

Melt butter in saucepan. Add cream cheese and stir until melted.

Add cream and spices and stir until smooth.

Add Parmesan and Romano cheeses slowly; be sure to stir constantly.

When mixture is smooth slowly add sour cream and ricotta cheese.

Boil and drain a package of lasagna noodles.

Cook, clean, and prepare seafood you want to use; I use crab, lobster, and shrimp, but you can add scallops, clams, or whatever you like.

Cheese for layering:

1 cup mozzarella cheese, shredded
1 cup cheddar cheese, shredded

You can adjust quantities based on taste.

Grease 9 x 13 baking pan. Layer in one layer of cooked noodles, seafood mixture, sauce, and cheese. Repeat so that the cheese layer is on the top.

Cook at 350 degrees until sauce is bubbly and cheese is lightly browned.

Note: This is not an inexpensive meal to make, so spurge and use a *good* quality cheese; the cheese really does make the difference.

Sloppy Joe Pasta

1 lb. ground beef
1 cup water
Sloppy Joe mix
8 oz. tomato sauce
6 oz. tomato paste
1 box macaroni (around 8 oz.), boiled and drained
2 cups shredded cheddar cheese

Brown ground beef. Add water, sloppy Joe mix, tomato sauce, and tomato paste. Cook until it thickens. Add the pasta to the meat mixture.

Put in greased baking dish. Cover with shredded cheese.

Bake at 350 degrees for 30–35 minutes.

Cranberry Bread

Submitted by Veronique Boudreau

2 cups flour
½ cup sugar
1 tbs. baking powder
½ tsp. salt
⅔ cup orange juice, fresh
2 eggs
3 tbs. butter
½ cup walnuts, chopped
1½ cup cranberries, chopped (I use Ocean Spray)
2 tsps. orange zest, grated

Preheat oven to 350 degrees. Grease an 8 or 9 x 4½ x 3 inch loaf pan.

Mix flour, sugar, baking powder, and salt in a large mixing bowl. Add orange juice, eggs, and butter until blended. *Don't* overmix.

Fold in walnuts, cranberries, and orange zest. Pour batter in pan and bake for 45–50 minutes (ovens will differ).

Cool in pan for 15 minutes and remove.

Allow to completely cool and wrap in tinfoil for a day.

Spaghetti Salad

Submitted by Janel Flynn

This was a recipe my Grandmother Crader made often. Everyone in the family loved it. It was very refreshing and was served often at picnics or potlucks.

1 lb. spaghetti (broken up and cooked; break before cooking)
1 lb. bottle Zesty Italian dressing
½ bottle Salad Supreme seasoning

Add together and chill overnight.

Next day add:

2 tomatoes, chopped
1 large onion, chopped
4–5 stalks celery, chopped
1 large green pepper, chopped
1 cucumber, sliced

Mix very well and serve.

Spaghetti and Meatballs

Submitted by Maureen Devlin-Murphy

This is a family favorite. I make it on Sunday once a month and we have family over for dinner. Serve with garlic bread and salad and it's a wonderful meal.

Sauce:
3 pork chops or pork steaks, lightly browned in olive oil
Onion finely chopped just as you turn the pork over
1 large can tomato juice or 2 large cans tomato sauce
1 cup red wine
2 cans broth (beef or chicken)
Garlic (lots), oregano, basil, and bay leaf to taste
2–3 tbs. sugar
2 cans tomato paste

Meatballs:
1 lb. ground beef
½ cup (or a little more—I dump) Parmesan cheese
5–6 slices of bread, slightly moistened (including crust)
1 tbs. garlic, granulated
1 tsp. (give or take, depending on your family) black pepper
1 egg

Lightly brown the pork in olive oil and add the finely chopped onions as you turn the pork over. Continue to brown, then add the tomato juice, wine, broth, and seasoning. This should simmer for at least an hour, then add tomato paste. Continue to simmer on very low flame.

While the sauce is simmering, prepare the meatballs: Mix all ingredients together and make into meatballs. (I usually smell it to see if I smell the garlic; if not . . . add more). Bake in the oven at 350 degrees for about 20 minutes. You can also fry the meatballs if you prefer. Add the meatballs to the sauce (after the tomato paste). Simmer with the meatballs at least an additional hour; the longer the better! (You may need to add a bit of water because the meatballs will soak up some of the liquid and the sauce will become thick.) Serve over your favorite pasta.

Mike's Favorite Chicken Pot Pie Casserole

Submitted by Vivian Shane

This is my husband's favorite meal. Whenever we have company for dinner he asks me to make this dish. I think he invites people over just so he can have this casserole!

1 can cream of chicken soup (10¾ oz.)
1 cup milk
½ tsp. seasoned salt
2 cups cooked chicken, cubed
16 oz. bag broccoli, carrots, and cauliflower, thawed and drained (I also like using sweet peas, broccoli, corn, and carrots)
1 cup cheddar cheese, shredded
1 cup (2.8 oz.) Durkee French Fried Onions
4 oz. pkg. refrigerator crescent rolls

Combine soup, milk, salt, chicken, veggies, one-half cup cheese, and one-half can onions. Place in 8 x 13 greased baking dish. Bake, covered, at 375 degrees for 20 minutes. Unwrap crescent rolls and separate into triangles and place on top of casserole. Bake, uncovered, 15 minutes longer. Top with remaining cheese and onions. Bake, uncovered, 3 to 5 minutes longer, or until onions are golden brown.

Ricotta Cheese Chocolate Chip Cookies

Submitted by Bobby Toby

This is not your typical chocolate chip cookie as there is no brown sugar.

4 cups flour
1½ tsps. baking soda
1¾ cups sugar
½ cup butter
3 eggs
1 lb. ricotta cheese
2 tsps. vanilla
1 bag chocolate chips

Mix flour and baking soda. Mix and cream sugar and butter. Beat three eggs and add to sugar mixture. Add ricotta cheese and then flour mixture. Add vanilla, then chips. Bake at 400 degrees 10–12 minutes.

Coconut Lime Pie

Submitted by Melissa Nicholson

My mom, Martha, would make this in the summer. She'd double the recipe and put it in a 9 x 13 cake pan. It keeps well in the freezer and tastes so yummy on a hot afternoon.

2 cups crushed graham crackers
¼ cup butter or margarine, melted
Red and green food coloring
Shaved coconut
8 oz. pkg. cream cheese, softened
14 oz. canned sweetened condensed milk
6 oz. canned frozen limeade, defrosted
4½ oz. Cool Whip, thawed

Mix the graham crackers with the melted butter and press into an 8 inch pie dish.

In a small bowl, mix red food coloring with the coconut flakes.
In mixer at high speed, beat cream cheese until creamy. Add condensed milk and mix until blended. Beat in limeade.
At low speed, add whipped topping and green food coloring and mix until blended.
Pour onto the crust. Sprinkle the red coconut flakes on top.
  Refrigerate at least 3 hours (I think it's best frozen).

Books by Kathi Daley

Come for the murder, stay for the romance.

Buy them on Amazon today.

Zoe Donovan Cozy Mystery:

Halloween Hijinks
The Trouble With Turkeys
Christmas Crazy
Cupid's Curse
Big Bunny Bump-off
Beach Blanket Barbie
Maui Madness
Derby Divas
Haunted Hamlet
Turkeys, Tuxes, and Tabbies
Christmas Cozy
Alaskan Alliance
Matrimony Meltdown – *April 2015*
Soul Surrender – *May 2015*
Heavenly Honeymoon – *June 2015*

Paradise Lake Cozy Mystery:

Pumpkins in Paradise
Snowmen in Paradise
Bikinis in Paradise
Christmas in Paradise
Puppies in Paradise

Whales and Tails Cozy Mystery:

Romeow and Juliet
The Mad Catter
Grimm's Furry Tail – *March 2015*

Road to Christmas Romance:

Road to Christmas Past

Kathi Daley lives with her husband, kids, grandkids, and Bernese mountain dogs in beautiful Lake Tahoe. When she isn't writing, she likes to read (preferably at the beach or by the fire), cook (preferably something with chocolate or cheese), and garden (planting and planning, not weeding). She also enjoys spending time on the water when she's not hiking, biking, or snowshoeing the miles of desolate trails surrounding her home.

Kathi uses the mountain setting in which she lives, along with the animals (wild and domestic) that share her home, as inspiration for her cozy mysteries.

Stay up to date with her newsletter, *The Daley Weekly*. There's a link to sign up on both her Facebook page and her website, or you can access the sign-in sheet at: http://eepurl.com/NRPDf

Visit Kathi:
Facebook at Kathi Daley Books,
www.facebook.com/kathidaleybooks

Kathi Daley Books Group Page –
https://www.facebook.com/groups/569578823146850/

Kathi Daley Recipe Exchange -
https://www.facebook.com/groups/752806778126428/

Webpage - www.kathidaley.com

E-mail - kathidaley@kathidaley.com

Recipe Submission E-mail –
kathidaleyrecipes@kathidaley.com

Goodreads:
https://www.goodreads.com/author/show/7278377.
Kathi_Daley

Twitter at Kathi Daley@kathidaley -
https://twitter.com/kathidaley

Tumblr - http://kathidaleybooks.tumblr.com/

Amazon Author Page -
http://www.amazon.com/Kathi-
Daley/e/B00F3BOX4K/ref=sr_tc_2_0?qid=141823
7358&sr=8-2-ent

Pinterest - http://www.pinterest.com/kathidaley/

38845523R00108

Made in the USA
Lexington, KY
27 January 2015